AND OTHER ENEMIES:
STORIES
OF CONSUMING
DESIRE

Cover design by Joan Wilking
Cover photo © Carol Kohen/The Image Bank
Special thanks to Larry Blake for copy editing

For information contact:
Essex Press
P.O. Box 914
North Andover, MA 01845

sxpress@banet.net
sxpress.freeservers.com

ISBN 0-9668972-4-2

"Yield" was previously published in *The American Scholar.*
"Fat Eyes" originally appeared in the spring 1996 issue of the
Emrys Journal, P.O. Box 8813, Greenville, SC 29604.

Printed in the United States of America

AND OTHER ENEMIES:
STORIES
OF CONSUMING
DESIRE

Edited by Leslie Powell

CONTENTS

Susan Thomas, Breakfast With Marylin   1

Gilbert Allen, Fat Eyes   12

E. K. Wilson & A-S. Kartsonis, Living The Sweet Life   23

Marylin Lytle Barr, Liquid Amber   30

Jeffrey Ihlenfeldt, Romanza   31

Beth Ann Fennelly, Why I Can't Cook For Your
          Self-Centered Architect Cousin   53

Donna Childs, Waiting   55

J. Warren Norton, illustration   60

Ron Pullins, Two Hunters' Tales   61

Denise Brennan Watson, False Charms & Chitlins   72

Dave Hendrickson, Yeah, But Can She Cook?   86

Marylin Lytle Barr, Musical Interlude   98

Beth Ann Fennelly, Yield   100

Estelle Jelinek, My Mother's Eating Lessons   102

June Brown, When Preacher Came To Supper   109

Marylin Lytle Barr, Rampion Season   114

Hollis Seamon, Blood Sugar   115

Anne E. Tremblay, Let Them Eat Cake   120

Marylin Lytle Barr, Rose Hip Puree   130

Pam Burris, Ingredients   130

Toni Amato, Barbecue   139

Toni Amato, Chocolate   141

Leslie Powell, Eat That   143

Amanda Kenny, Yo-Yo Girl   165

David Tillman, War Fare   172

Ben Wilensky, The Bezaloo   180

Introduction

Food—it's good for us; it keeps us alive. If only it were so simple: we eat, we live, we thrive. And yet we know the dark side of food: food as our enemy, prone to excess or scarcity. Like the lover we can't live without, food forces us to walk the tightrope of wanting too much and getting too little.

It's no surprise that food and desire—two elements that permeate our all too human natures—should be linked in our psyche, our spirits, and our bodies. Our behavior, as well as our mythology, bears out the connection. From our hunger for love to our Biblical Eve, whom we still blame for eating the Forbidden Fruit and losing us to paradise, we still deny ourselves food as a way to heaven. And as a way to get thin and find love.

In this eclectic and entertaining set of stories, essays, and poems about food, don't look for the obvious. You'll find no diets or exercise programs here.

What these writers offer is more complicated and more necessary: a beacon to look at ourselves and our relation to others through the simple ritual of gathering, preparing, and eating food.

As with all good stories, these peel back the layers of the ordinary and give us a clearer view of who we are and how we got here.

Besides food, there is an enemy at the heart of many of these stories. The enemies come in many forms—family members, lovers, friends, even aliens and doughboys.

So pull up a chair, tuck in your napkin, and nourish yourself with a variety of writing: poignant, funny, sorrowful, joyful, exuberant, and wise. We've cooked up something for every appetite. Enjoy.

Leslie Powell

BREAKFAST WITH MARILYN

We always sat in the back booth, hidden by the curve of the aqua blue Formica counter. It was just the two of us and Jackie, the fat waitress. Nobody else was ever there early on Saturday mornings; the garment district was empty. Only my father and a few other people were in the building.

The coffee shop was on the ground floor of 498 Seventh Avenue. I used to ride to work with my father on Saturdays so I could get to my ballet class at ten o'clock.

I never figured out why she was there. I think she had a friend with a business in the building. We didn't talk about what she did when she wasn't sitting in the back booth of the coffee shop. What we talked about was food.

We were both on diets. Mine was new. I was counting calories with one of those little wheels you got in drugstores. You dialed the food on the outside of the wheel and a little window on the inside told you how many calories it had. I was trying to keep my daily consumption down to 900.

I wasn't fat yet, but I wanted to be a ballet dancer and I had more curve than I was supposed to. I had just hit puberty. My ballet teacher had already looked disapprovingly at my rounded hips and my peach-sized breasts. Plums were the approved size for a dancer. In class once, my teacher had corrected my extension and turnout, but couldn't get my leg any higher because my hip got in the way. He

1

patted the hip twice then, like it was something I shouldn't bring to class.

She was on a diet because her body was famous. It had to be perfect. Not too thin, and certainly not fat. It didn't have to fit a form dictated by technique and line. It just had to be inviting, ripe, tantalizing in every way. It had to be the body people recognized as hers.

I never talked about who she was. Not to her or to anyone else. It seemed as though it would be impolite, like pointing a finger or name-dropping. And anyway, she wasn't really the person I'd seen in magazines or movies. She wasn't even someone you'd notice in a crowd. She blended into the coffee shop like the napkins, the paper place mats, like the little pitchers of milk and bowls of sugar on each table.

She always sat on the kitchen side of the U-shaped counter, while I sat on the other side near the door. Jackie bumped around in the open space between us, taking our orders, serving, wiping, refilling our cups. One Saturday Jackie had a twisted ankle, wrapped in a messy Ace bandage. She was trying not to walk on it, so she asked me to move from my side of the counter to the other, where the sad-looking woman was sitting.

"You know who she is, right?" Jackie whispered.

I nodded.

"OK, then. Keep it to yourself and don't bother her. Got it?"

"Sure," I said.

Actually, until Jackie brought it up I hadn't recognized her. She wore a head scarf, usually, and sunglasses. But even when she took off the disguise, she was so small and colorless in her tan raincoat, so drab with her pale eyes and pale lips, her pale hair, that who she was hadn't occurred to me. Movie stars were flamboyant, splashy, bigger than life. In movies her huge blue eyes, bright red lips, and undulating body filled every inch of the screen. Even black-and-white still photographs of her bulged with desire.

I remembered seeing pictures of her in the newspaper the summer before, when she had a miscarriage. The photos showed her looking wan and desperate. But here, in the coffee shop, she looked very young. Nowhere near my age, but not like an adult woman. And she looked like she could break.

I sat down on a stool five or six places away from her and looked over the items on the menu and in the display case. What I usually had was a bagel and coffee, but what I always really wanted was a Danish. I dialed it up on my calorie counter—357 calories for a cheese Danish! 325 for prune. 295 for cherry. I began to feel depressed. Even the bagel was too many calories, and that was dry. Forget about butter or cream cheese. I was thirteen years old and already I felt my life was over. How did people live like this?

I dialed again. Grape-nut flakes. Yecch, but I could do it. But with milk, even skim milk, they were over the limit. Then I tried everything in the display case. Jell-O came in at a trim and sylphlike 43 calories.

"Red Jell-O," I told Jackie.

"Take the green," she said. "They made it yesterday. You want the whipped cream?"

"Yeah," I said, and then I remembered. "Actually, no, thanks."

The Jell-O arrived and I watched it sway over the top of the parfait glass. I sighed. It was my destiny. When it stopped moving I lifted my spoon.

The woman turned on her stool to face me.

"You must excuse me for speaking," she said. She used the same slow, air-filled voice she used in the movies. "But I couldn't help noticing what you ordered for breakfast, and..." She paused for breath. "I just can't bear not saying anything." She paused again, panting a little and looking at the Jell-O. "I know I'm interfering, honey, but..."

"That's OK.," I said.

"Well, do you mind," she said, "if I move over a few stools?"

3

I shook my head.

She glared at my Jell-O and I patted it with my spoon. It jiggled. She lifted her spoon. "May I?"

"Be my guest." I shrugged.

She touched it on one side and then on the other. The Jell-O bobbled to both sides, then shivered.

I gave it a little tap, and then she did. We took turns playing with it for a minute or two. We were having a pretty good time. The Jell-O was plopping and splooshing and we were laughing.

Jackie came back out of the kitchen and limped over. She looked down at me. "What are you *really* going to have for breakfast?"

Marilyn said, "Give her what I always have. It'll be good for her."

Jackie looked at me.

I nodded OK.

"It's the best breakfast when you're on a diet," she said. "And I know you're on a diet. I saw you dialing that silly doo-hickey that counts calories."

I gave the little wheel a spin.

"I'm always on a diet," she said. "I guess you could say I've become an expert." Her eyes were so blue and so sad-looking. "And you know," she looked over at me. "I've tried everything."

It was Jackie who suggested we move from the counter to the back table. The next Saturday she no longer wore the ankle bandage, but she was still limping. "This way," she said, indicating the back booth, "you'll be close by and I can clean the whole counter. Besides, it's more private."

We both looked at Marilyn.

She frowned. "Boy oh boy. Who'd think we'd get in so much trouble for playing with Jell-O?"

Marilyn ordered the usual. Black coffee, half a grapefruit, poached eggs on dry wheat toast, and a scoop of cottage cheese.

I said I'd have the same thing.

Marilyn patted my hand. "I think you're doing the right thing. You'll see, it'll give you lots of energy and the pounds will come right off, as long as this is your biggest meal."

How could I tell her about dinner, when I went out with my grandparents to the same restaurant every week? I couldn't tell the waiter, Pasquale, "Just a glass of water please, and some string beans."

Even lunch presented problems. I had a ten o'clock ballet class and a character class at one, followed by another ballet class at three. I was always ravenous by noon, and at two-thirty I could easily eat the piano. Everyone else brought an apple and a yogurt for lunch, and an orange or a banana for later. Sometimes we went out for Cokes or an orangeade.

I'd bring the yogurt and apple with me, but it always seemed like such a heartless lunch. What I really wanted was the Hamburger Express across the street, where the burger and fries came chugging down the counter on a tiny freight train. Occasionally, I'd sneak across the street just to watch the trains and smell the delightfully greasy aroma. A few times I actually sat down and ordered. Later, I'd go back early to class and throw it up in the bathroom before anyone else came in.

The next week she asked me what I'd brought for lunch that day. I reached into my ballet bag, under the leotards, tights, leg warmers, socks, ballet slippers, pointe shoes, towel, liniment, hairbrush, and hairpins, and I pulled out the yogurt and apple.

"Now that's just perfect," she said. "Lots of protein and vitamins. And just think, only a hundred calories in that apple."

"How many in the yogurt?" I asked. I'd never considered it had calories. I didn't even like it.

"Oh, stop worrying," she said. "You'll knock it off dancing. You need to get all that calcium. And they're both white, my favorite."

"An apple?" I said. "Looks red to me."

"Well, silly, bite into it," she said. "Then what color is it?"

She had me there.

"How come you like white food so much?" I asked her the next Saturday.

"Funny, isn't it?" she said. "I like white. I think white simplifies everything." She rested her face on her hands. "Things can get pretty complicated sometimes. My shrink says I have to learn to accept my contradictory impulses. The only trouble is, I get so mixed up I end up bleary and depressed and then I can't even sleep. I have trouble sleeping."

"I know what you mean," I said. "I do too."

"Gee," she said. "At your age. That's too bad." She patted my shoulder sympathetically and noticed the clock. "Oops," she said, "I better skedaddle. I have an appointment downtown in half an hour."

Then I didn't see her for a few weeks. My father got sick and didn't work Saturdays for a while, so I took a bus to the city and the subway directly to class. I wasn't losing much weight, either. It was so unfair. My best friend brought two sandwiches to school every day, a cheese or salami and one chicken or tuna salad or her favorite lobster salad, plus a triangle of Swiss Knight cheese and two cookies or a Hostess cupcake. She never gained an ounce. I ate these stupid apples every day and yogurt on gym days or when I had a ballet class. I never got any thinner and I was always hungry.

My father said it was my metabolism; I inherited it from him. My father weighed over three hundred pounds. He was six-foot-one, though, and he could carry it. He had a handsome face and was really smart. People noticed he was fat, but it wasn't the main thing. And—he wasn't a ballet dancer.

My mother was always at me to eat less and to try all these diet things, like Flav-r-straws, these gross drinking straws with saccharine inside of them that were supposed to make skim milk taste like chocolate or strawberry milkshakes. I mean, God! Why didn't she try them! But she stayed reasonably thin no matter what she ate. I mean it. Candy—God, all underneath my parents' king-size bed was candy. Wall-to-wall chocolate bars and pistachio nuts, so my mom could snack at night while she was watching TV in her bedroom, waiting for my father to come home at eleven with a hot fudge sundae. She never gave me or my middle brother any of her stash because she was afraid we had my father's metabolism. But my youngest brother, her favorite, seemed to have inherited her body-type, so he was allowed to watch TV with her and share her candy.

The Saturday my father went back to work I found Marilyn sitting at our booth in the coffee shop drinking her black coffee. It was the only non-whitish thing I ever saw her have.

I told Jackie what I wanted, and while she brought Marilyn's breakfast I took out a strip of these pills my mother had gotten me. You were supposed to take the green ones in the morning, the yellow ones at noon, and the pink ones at night.

Marilyn looked horrified. "Where did you get those?" she said.

I told her my mother got them for me so I could lose weight.

"Who gave them to her?"

"Our family doctor," I said. What was her problem?

"Did he know that they were for you?"

"Sure, I was standing right there."

"Well, it's wrong," she said. "He made a mistake. You shouldn't take them. You're just a kid."

"I'm mature for my age."

She had the grace to smile and pat my hand. It was a lovely smile, but her worry came through.

"What's wrong with them?" I asked her.

"Believe me, honey, I *know*. I told you. I've tried *everything*. They're amphetamines. They make you real jumpy. Too jumpy even to sleep." She chewed her lip. "I don't want to scare you. I'm sorry. I had a bad night again last night. I didn't sleep at all."

I said, "You know, I've been talking nonstop, even in class. My muscles twitch all night and I can't stop thinking of all these ridiculous things, like science projects, history dates, math problems, student council candidates and their campaign managers."

"See?" she said, excited. "That's exactly what I mean. Are you going to stop taking them?"

"Well," I said, "I did lose five pounds this week."

I managed to lose about fifteen pounds. But after I stopped the pills I gained back five, even though I was still on the two-grapefruits-and-a-steak-twice-a-day diet. I had expected to be prettier, more glamorous. But I was still the same old me, with a better figure.

One Saturday a man came into the coffee shop. He sat down at the counter near the outside door, a big guy, in his forties, a truck driver or a shipping clerk, maybe. He picked up the menu for a second and then he put it down.

Jackie went over, took his order, and waddled back to the kitchen. He glanced at us, me and Marilyn, two girls in a back booth wearing sweat shirts, jeans, and sneakers, no makeup, our hair pulled back in ponytails. Hers was white-blond and wispy, only a tiny bit of hair pulled into a rubber band. Mine was brown and thick, puffed tight and high on my head so my eyes turned up at the comers. He glanced at us and looked away.

Marilyn scrinched her face. "Hey," she said. "Want to see something?"

"What?" I asked.

"Her," she said. "You know. Want to see her?"

She was getting excited, working her upper lip and tongue. She wet her lips, sat up straight, and arched her back. Then she lifted her head and looked, eyes wide and focused, at the man across the counter.

She was a different person. Her pale skin glowed. Every feature in her face was larger, she was taller, her bones were more distinct. Everything about her seemed to vibrate.

The man looked up at us again, and dropped his jaw. His eyes bulged, face turned red. Marilyn smiled at him, held his gaze a moment, and turned to me, giggling.

"See?" she said. "It's easy."

The next week I waited for her until nine o'clock. I knew I was going to miss my first ballet class. She had told us she was going to California soon to make another movie, a comedy about the roaring twenties, but she wasn't leaving right away. Finally I ordered a cheese Danish and a coffee. Jackie looked at me in disbelief, but she brought it and I ate the whole thing. Then I went to the bathroom, but not the one in the coffee shop that's just for one person. I went to the big one in the lobby of the building, with marble stalls, high ceilings, and lots of air. Everything you did in there echoed like crazy.

I was just finishing throwing up the cheese Danish when someone else came in, which was weird, because the building was almost empty and I had Jackie's key.

"Is that you, honey?" her voice said.

I knew it was her. I could see her white sneakers with no socks.

"How'd you get in?" I asked.

"Ricardo had the master key," she said.

"Ricardo?"

"The elevator man. What's going on in there? Are you OK.?"

Yeah, I was thinking, I'm starting to get good at this. I'm going to be very good at this.

I flushed and opened the stall door. She looked at me from over by the sink and her face was very old, suddenly, at least ten years older than before.

She put her arms around me. "It's not worth it," she said.

"Nobody's worth it."

"But it is," I said. "You feel so clean afterwards, like nothing is inside you."

"I know," she said. "You feel like nothing has ever happened to you. It's like being born. You're starting all over with no mistakes."

I never saw her again, and a few years later I was in the corps de ballet of a small company. We were performing some crazy Armenian ballet at the La Perq Space of the Brooklyn Academy of Music, and during the intermission I heard that she had died, a suicide probably.

For some reason I had never told anyone about Marilyn. I guess I thought nobody would believe me, or maybe I just wanted to keep her for myself. I felt so terrible, as though I had really lost somebody important to me.

We all went out to a coffee shop after the performance. The soloist in the company was going on and on about all the jobs she had been offered in Europe. The Stuttgart Company wanted her, she said, and Frankfurt, and Roland Petit in Paris, and blah, blah, blah.

I sat there while she went on and on. My stomach was growling and I felt so totally empty. I ordered coffee, poached eggs and dry wheat toast, a half grapefruit and a scoop of cottage cheese, the one meal I can always keep down. The one meal that still always satisfies me.

While I was waiting for the food to come, a really cute guy walked into the coffee shop. He looked at all of us in our fading stage makeup and long hair all Brilliantined, but loose now, hanging down our backs, and his eyes fastened on Pixie, the soloist. She was still babbling about her great auditions.

Suddenly I sat up and arched my back. I moistened my lips, lifted my head, and focused my eyes on the cute guy until he stared at me.

Glamour. It's that easy.

Susan Thomas lives in Vermont where she writes, grows, and eats whatever she can. She has an MFA from Sarah Lawrence College, where she studied fiction with Grace Paley. Her poems and stories have appeared in over sixty journals, including *Nimrod, Kalliope, Columbia, Feminist Studies,* and *The Atlanta Review,* and her collection of short stories was a finalist for the Bakeless Prize for Fiction last year. Her poem "The Murdered Girl" won the 1999 Editor's Prize from the *Spoon River Poetry Review,* a story, "Dangers of Descent" won first prize from *New York Stories* 1999 Fiction Contest.

Although she is not the girl in this story, for three months in 1957 when she was eleven years old, Susan actually did eat breakfast in the same coffee shop as Marilyn Monroe.

FAT EYES

After her father phoned from the hospital, Harriet couldn't look at the country-cured hams without crying. Since he weighed nearly as much as she did—three hundred pounds—the doctors had decided to keep Henry for "observation," even though his heart monitor was putting the timer for the new deep-fat fryer to shame. Then and there, Harriet promised to spend more time *observing* them both.

At one-thirty, when the lunch stampede had dwindled to a few strays grazing at the salad bar, she told Marcus, the assistant manager of Karrie's Kountry Kookhouse, that she'd be taking her two-week vacation "starting right now." She'd look in on Henry during visiting hours, mornings and evenings, and use the rest of her time to get started on the PoundsAway Program. She'd seen it advertised on the place mats at the restaurant for the past month. RESULTS GUARANTEED! LOSE THE WEIGHT! WAIT TO PAY!

"Baby, you're not fat," Marcus said. "You're just—*comfortable*."

"Not like you," she said. "I'm no La-Z-Boy."

Marcus threw her grin right back at her. "I never had no chair in mind, Harriet." He patted the worn red vinyl of the empty booth. "More like a love seat."

How did black men ever get such great teeth? She untied her apron and tossed it onto the Formica. "Dream on, honey." Too bad Marcus was married.

PoundsAway (Incorporated) stuck out in the new strip mall on the east side of town, sandwiched between a florist and a Sara Lee outlet store. The glass doors opened with the wink of an electric eye, just like at the Winn Dixie. Except for the Weigh Station with a digital scale, it was one big open room lined with mirrors that hung like icicles down to the gray industrial carpet.

They'd told her the details over the phone. You paid one dollar for every pound you lost until you hit your goal weight. Then you went on Maintenance for at least a year, and, for the incentive, paid a little extra for whatever you gained back. They took her MasterCard number and said that programs started on the hour, nine to five, Mondays through Saturdays.

Now it was almost five o'clock. About two dozen women were hovering around the scale, most of them skinny as hummingbirds, shivering in leotards. Harriet was glad she'd decided to wear a fleece warm-up suit. It might have been the middle of March, but it still felt colder inside the building than out in the parking lot.

She decided to approach the one woman dressed in something Harriet might have found in her own closet. The name tag said MARGARET. "Why are they all wearing bedroom slippers?" Harriet whispered.

"Maintenance girls. Gotta make their goal weight every week. Weigh over, pay over. Ten dollars a pound. Five dollars a shoe." Margaret's laugh sounded more like a sneeze. "You learn to choose your clothes real careful around here."

"Couldn't they bring a coat?"

"If it goes through the door, it goes on the scale. Corporate policy."

Harriet fingered the name tag on her own jacket.

"Oh, you did good for the first time, sugar. It'll just add to your base weight. That way you'll have a few ounces to play with later on."

A buzzer sounded. One of the mirrors on the far side of the

room opened from the back. A frizzy redhead appeared in the shortest shorts Harriet had ever seen. Harriet stared at her thighs, then looked down at her own arms glumly. It was no contest.

"Hi. My name's Bambi, and I'll be y'all's Loss Facilitator for today." She adjusted the Wonderbra under her tank top, then clapped her hands once. "Time to get our meat on the hoof, ladies."

The skinniest women began to line up in front of the scale. Harriet and Margaret fell in at the end, where they couldn't see what Bambi was doing.

"Excellent!" Bambi said. "Ladies, what do we say?"

"Aaaaah."

Harriet began to wonder if she should report her credit card stolen—as of yesterday. Then she looked at Margaret. She wasn't thin, but she didn't look fat either, at least not by Harriet's standards. "How much've you lost since you started?"

"Me? Two hundred and fifty pounds."

Harriet felt her heart flutter.

Margaret grimaced. "That's twenty-five pounds, ten times. I'm glad my husband can afford it."

The *ooooohs* were leading the *aaaaahs* by about three to one. Most of the Maintenance girls weren't making their goal weights. Bambi had to go to the Weigh Station desk for extra credit-card slips.

The line finally shrunk to Harriet. "First time?" Bambi said.

Harriet nodded as she placed her left foot on the scale, then slowly raised her right one to join it.

"Three-oh-four. Congratulations, Harriet!" Bambi handed her a red-and-white 32-ounce plastic cup with a straw sticking out of the top. It said MOST AMBITIOUS LOSER in block letters. "Your personalized diet will arrive in the mail next week. Until then, just remember—water has no calories! Drink whenever you feel hungry!"

Bambi told the rest of the women to form a circle, then

cartwheeled into the center. She stood on her hands while she spoke. "Now that I've got y'all's attention, today we're going to work on self-denial."

Margaret's knee nudged Harriet's. "Two face lifts and a BMW and she's an expert on self-denial. Wait'll you hear about how she lost seven pounds for her balance-beam dismount."

"Portion control," the inverted Bambi continued. "That's the key to Lifestyle Management! Now I'll need a volunteer." She sprang to her feet and stared squarely at Harriet. "Who's our resident expert on portions?"

Harriet felt like a horseshoe magnet surrounded by an army of compass needles.

"Well, I work in Karrie's Kountry Kookhouse. I make them up all the time."

"Excellent!" Bambi said. "We eat what we see. We become what we eat." She took Harriet by the elbow and led her to the nearest mirror. "We see what we become." Bambi faced the group and pointed her thumb backward over her shoulder. "Harriet is living proof."

Bambi took a Ziploc bag and a postal scale out of the Weigh Station desk drawer.

"Sliced turkey breast," Harriet said. "You'd better refrigerate that."

"It's for demonstration purposes," Bambi said. "We won't be *eating* anything." Even when she frowned, the ends of her mouth still pointed upward. She handed Harriet the Ziploc bag but kept the small scale on her side of the Weigh Station. "Give me an ounce, Harriet. One ounce."

"I don't know if I can." Harriet felt herself blushing. She'd failed algebra in high school, twice. "I never was very good with numbers."

Bambi sighed. "Whatever you'd put on a sandwich."

Harriet took out the customary Karrie's portion for a Club Special, then lifted off one slice—then one more—to put back into the bag. "There," she said.

Her brown eyes dilating, Bambi walked backward to the mirrored door, then disappeared. She returned with somebody who looked like Dolly Parton before she'd hit puberty.

"What did I tell you, Melanie?"

Melanie's platinum hairdo moved slowly, from side to side. "Sweet Jesus, you're right! Those are the *fattest* eyes I've ever seen!"

Bambi dropped the loose turkey slices on the postal scale and waited for it to finish wobbling. "Four and a half ounces. What do we say, ladies?"

"Oooooh."

"See y'all next week," Bambi said.

Bambi stopped Harriet on her way out. "Maybe it's a *perceptual* problem. Maybe it has nothing to do with your *character*."

Harriet had planned to drive straight to the hospital, but she decided to go to her father's empty house instead. Her mother had died in her wheelchair of a brain aneurysm three years ago, in keeping with her conviction that women never had heart attacks—they were too busy giving them away. Harriet threw her MOST AMBITIOUS LOSER cup against the microwave oven. For one of the few times in her life, Harriet envied her mother—all one hundred and thirty-three pounds of her, safely underground, embalmed in her own Southern Comfort, where she couldn't cause any more damage.

Harriet hoped that her father hadn't done his laundry before feeling those chest pains on Thursday. But the hamper was empty. Then she walked back into the kitchen. The poor man had even emptied the dishwasher before driving himself to the hospital.

Her teeth had been clenched for the whole fifteen minutes since PoundsAway. They still were. She had to do *something*. So she gathered her father's clean shirts from the master bedroom closet and carried them downstairs on their hangers. Ironing, she'd decided, might even be better than washing for letting off steam.

The old ironing board stood next to the washer-dryer. When Harriet grabbed for the slender chain that had just brushed against her face, the overhead light didn't come on. She kept pulling and letting go, listening to it clicking, till she finally reached up to re-move the bulb. But it was only loose in the socket, not burned out. After she turned it clockwise, it almost blinded her.

She looked down and rubbed the spots from her eyes. "First thing gone right today."

Trying not to smile, she smoothed the iron over the checkered shirt. She enjoyed the scent of the steam. It reminded her of cook-ing, without the calories. In twenty minutes she put the last shirt back on its hanger, admiring the crisp collar that would never come straight out of a dryer, no matter what the label said. She felt better. And she skipped supper for the first time she could remember.

From the open doorway, he looked asleep. "Henry?" Ever since Harriet's mother had died, her father had insisted she call him by his first name. "How're you feeling?"

"It's only 'cause I'm a veteran," he said, opening his eyes and waving his big right hand over the bedsheets. "That's why I'm still here. Friggin' commies."

Harriet grabbed his wrist to slow him down. She didn't want him pulling out his IV. "That's silly," she said.

"I got benefits, see? Good benefits. They know Uncle Sam's gonna take care of me, right down to the box he'll bury me in. If I was just Medicare, they'd've kicked my butt outta here this morning." He shoved the bedrail with his foot. "They know. A nurse even called me Sergeant."

Harriet smiled. Her father complained the way some people played five Bingo cards at once on Wednesday nights. "You still haven't told me how you're feeling."

"Like I got a sandbag on my chest." He snickered. "But I think it's taking a leak. I walked around the whole floor after lunch. Didn't even lean on the wall."

"Great."

"Last night they said my major arteries looked like LA during an earthquake. They didn't know I could hear." He shook his head. "I guess they need a laugh too. Job must get damn depressing. Dealing with fat jerks like me."

Harriet blushed for them both. Then she told him she'd started her program at PoundsAway. "Maybe you'd like to read these brochures," Harriet said, cautiously putting them under the case for his reading glasses. "They make a lot of sense, Henry."

"*Snacking on the Hoof. Feeding Your Guilt. Drowning Your Fat.* Read this? My goldfish are dying, and I'm supposed to worry about drowning my fat?"

"I fed them," Harriet said. "I just came from the house."

"Bless you," he said. "Eat a cheeseburger for me. They're in the freezer."

"Which one?" She wasn't planning to eat it, but at least she could throw it out to make him feel better.

"Upstairs. Cheeseburgers in Paradise. I only keep the stuff from the hunting trips downstairs." He gave her his best laugh of the day. "Went through Hell to get it. Figure it should stay there."

For the next week, Harriet kept her water cup in plain sight, vacuumed the carpets three times a day (for the exercise), and slept at her father's house. She stayed in her own bedroom—the one she couldn't remember ever *not* knowing, though the family had actually moved in when she was two and a half, almost thirty-five years ago. The bed hadn't seemed so small then. It held the whole world— her Barbies, her Ken, her stuffed Bullwinkle, even her friend, Mary, a sweet, gap-toothed girl who'd sneak inside to use it as a trampoline.

Harriet bit her lip. Whenever she filled her cup at the Frigidaire, she'd open the freezer and stare at the cheeseburgers, individually wrapped, stacked like old 45s in a jukebox. She'd stick the straw between her teeth and suck deeply. *Portion control. We eat what we see.* Today, she shut her eyes and closed the door. She'd have to weigh in again the day after tomorrow.

She sucked more water, then sniffed suspiciously. Something seemed to float over the potpourri that she'd put on the kitchen table. She checked the vegetable bins and found two withered apples and a soft potato with a black bottom. She double-wrapped them in plastic grocery bags and threw them into the garbage pail.

When she came back from her morning visit to the hospital, the smell was still there—only more so. She checked the bags—they didn't seem to be leaking. Squatting on her knees in the dining room, she sniffed the carpet. The scent was stronger but coming from no place in particular. Maybe your sense of smell got better when you ate less. She'd already cracked 300 naked pounds on the bathroom scale.

She decided that putting Lysol into the toilets and sinks might help. Her father stored all the cleaning supplies downstairs. When she opened the door to the basement, she gagged. The stairwell light flickered and popped, so she had to step slowly in darkness, holding her breath, listening to the wooden stairs creaking beneath her.

Groping her way to the laundry room, she could feel her feet sticking to the concrete. She breathed through her mouth as shallowly as she could. When she pulled the light chain, the bulb dimmed and wavered almost as soon as it went on. A soft whirring began from the concrete wall behind her.

In daylight the puddles might have been brown or red. The biggest one sat at the bottom of the freezer. She opened the door— then kicked it shut, coughing, leaving a bloody footprint under the handle.

This is what we eat. This is what we become.

"Calm down, Harriet. Come on, just spit it out."

She stammered about the stench, the blood, the soggy mess still in the freezer.

"Were you downstairs before?"

She sniffled. "I ironed your shirts last week."

"Did you turn off the light? With the chain?"

She nodded.

"It's the only good socket in the basement now. That's why I loosen the bulb. So the freezer keeps running."

She knelt on the linoleum squares and put her head on the bed-sheets, sobbing. "I'm sorry, Daddy. I'm so sorry."

"Hey there," he said, patting the crown of her head. "It's just an old deer I shot three years ago. Could have died a natural death by now."

"The smell," Harriet said. "You can't imagine it."

"Just throw everything into some Heftys and hose down the floor. Use the Wet Vac to suck it up."

"Can I put some bleach in the water?"

"Sure, honey. As much as you want." He lifted her chin with the tip of his finger. "Okay?"

She could still feel her shoulders shaking. "The body, Henry," she said. "Where should I bury it?"

"The trash, honey. Put it in the trash."

"The garbagemen won't take it. It's disgusting, it's—oh God, those women stare at me like I'm some kind of animal."

Now he held her face in both his hands. "You're my baby," he said. She could still see the scab from his IV line. "Did I ever tell you you got named after me?"

"After you?"

"That's right. Henry. Harry. Harriet. Your mom and me—well, we didn't always fight. We got along good, before the accident. You should've seen her. Anyway, we were *sure* you were gonna be a boy.

Don't ask me how. And she wanted to name you after me. She insisted. And you know how your mother got when she insisted on anything."

"God, yes," Harriet said.

"So you were Little Henry for six months. Boy, were we surprised."

She was still crying, but she laughed anyway.

"Harriet was my idea." He wiped her cheek with the corner of his bedsheet. "After a few weeks, we wondered why we ever wanted a boy. You should've seen the look in your mom's eyes whenever she fed you." He smiled. "Things have a way of working out. Just stay away from those skinny little bitches." He picked up *Drowning Your Fat* from the nightstand and Frisbeed it through the open doorway of the bathroom. "Did I hit the toilet for once?"

"Almost," she laughed. "Almost, Henry."

Harriet couldn't even think about sleeping until she'd cleaned up the basement. She found a dust mask next to the paint brushes, which cut the stench if she kept her breaths short and shallow.

It took her till four o'clock in the morning. She felt proud of herself. The garbagemen would be coming at dawn—she hadn't wanted the neighborhood dogs and cats to be tempted for a whole week before the next pickup. And after the bleach and the Wet Vac, the basement smelled more like a swimming pool than a slaughterhouse.

Now it didn't seem worth going to sleep. She had her instant coffee—no sugar, no cream, plenty of hot water—and waited for the garbage truck to make its morning rounds.

Then she decided to weigh in a day early.

She took a Ziploc bag from the kitchen cabinet and walked outside to the curb. She held her breath and untwisted the plastic tie. Then, she took out the biggest piece she could find, a shoulder roast still dripping in Handi-Wrap, and shoved it inside the small bag.

Inside her father's house, Harriet ran her fingernail along the raised seam, just to make sure it was perfect. *Doe, a deer, a female deer....* Let's see her slice off an ounce from *this*. And when doe-eyed Bambi tells her it stinks, it's disgraceful, it's disgusting, she'll just *oooooh* and ask her to have a little more respect—for her relations.

Gilbert Allen received his M.F.A. and Ph.D. from Cornell University, where he was a Ford Foundation Fellow. He currently teaches at Furman University, His poems, stories, and essays have appeared in *The American Scholar, College English, Cumberland Poetry Review, Emrys Journal, The Georgia Review, Image, Quarterly West, Shenandoah, The Southern Review,* and *The Tampa Review.* His three collections of poems are *In Everything* (Lotus, 1982), *Second Chances* (Orchises, 1991), and *Commandments at Eleven* (Orchises, 1994).

Eliot Kahlil Wilson and
Ariana-Sophia Kartsonis

LIVING THE SWEET LIFE

> *To comprehend a nectar*
> *Requires sorest need.*
> *— Emily Dickinson*

This is how they will find me. First, one brown shoe will float to the surface, and, later that day, workers will find my other brown shoe. This will start a storm of recrimination. Memos will appear in the employee dressing rooms: "Product contamination is grounds for immediate dismissal." A day, maybe two days, will pass.

A pair of chocolate socks will rise to the surface. Management will be furious. There will be serious talk of installing cameras and television monitors. It won't be until my boxer shorts, steaming and covered in a rich dark chocolate, float up to the surface that the full extent of my particular crime, in all of its delicious horror, comes to light. Kevorkian be damned. I've given it a great deal of thought. When the time comes, I'm ending my life by leaping into one of the giant copper cauldrons of liquid chocolate at Hershey Park in Hershey, Pennsylvania. What better way to die? A serotonin ecstasy. A warm, sweet sleep in a fattening, brown Jesus.

I can see my body spread out on the cooling board like a giant, ill-starred Keebler Elf.

Jack Sprat could eat no fat
His wife could eat no lean
So betwixt them both, you see
They licked the platter clean

There is a table in heaven, a long table filled with dish after dish of full-fat, lipid-laden, anything-but-diet foods; and women of every shape and size with full plates. None of them hate their bodies. None of heaven's girls assault themselves in a full-length mirror. No punching at saddlebags—real or imagined. No turning sideways and smacking hard at a curved abdomen.

Heaven is calorie-free. There is no vocabulary for low-fat, sugarless, cholesterol-free.

"Can you imagine," says one woman. "Back there, we looked at a menu and ruled out those foods that we really wanted but couldn't have. Then we chose from the one or two items left while all around us luscious foods arrived and sat themselves down in front of somebody else."

Yes, we told our friends, our husbands, ourselves, I actually prefer this plate of boiled dinner (hold the dressing) to fettuccine alfredo. I'd really rather eat Brer Rabbit's Delight while you eat thick-crusted, double-cheese, extra sausage, double pepperoni pizza. Just that melted mozzarella and garlic smell of pizza is plenty for me. I eat vicariously.

Yes, I love taking ten minutes to place an order. "How is this prepared? Dressing on the side. Just vinegar, no oil. Hold the butter. Hold the mayo. Hold the whole entree and begin again."

At that table in heaven we order cravings first. The ten-story stack of pancakes please. The banana split. The delicious freedom.

A Slice of Heaven

"It's called *Death by Chocolate,*" she says as she pushes toward me a gooey divot of cake that is so huge it looks as if they cut it with a post hole digger. We're at a local café drinking overpriced coffee and trying to breathe through a wool blanket of smoke. This piece of cake beckons to me. Although I'm a diabetic, I take a fork full from the heel of the cake and raise it up to the light. This is a magic moment for most people. There should be celestial music playing, but in the glimmer of icing on that cake I see kidney failure and the ensuing years of dialyses, I see distal neuropathy and nonhealing foot ulcers, I see heart disease. I see myself dying slowly like a stump. I also see not seeing. I'm already losing my vision. Tiny capillaries in one eye have already burst and stained sections of my visual field. Think of a windshield that never gets clean. Knowing this is something heavy everyday. That pain in my lower back isn't my back either. It's my kidneys talking: they're not happy, but the cake, the cake is delicious.

Take the Cake

It's Saturday afternoon and we decide to go out for coffee and a treat. It's taken 10 years for me to learn that I can eat the occasional slice of cake and with the right proportion of motion to consumption, I won't balloon into my former shape. So I order a slice of Death by Chocolate, a dark and fudgy wedge of sin, and settle down with my coffee and this slice of cake the size of a small building. Then, as my fork is poised to take down a full wing of that structure, the frosting glistens and in that glistening I see the cover of this month's Mademoiselle—a woman with bony wings for shoulder blades and a lyre for a breast bone. I see me as I once saw myself—shapeless and blob-like, floating on the margins of my life. Though I've yet to taste it, I know it won't be nearly as sweet now. It's an ambiguous indulgence, at best, a bittersweet bit of contraband.

I'm eight and I cannot see out of my left eye. I'm sporting a sweaty eye patch; a red bandanna covers my shaved head. My left hand is a hard plastic hook. My right hand grips a heavy plastic pumpkin. Though the strap is cutting into my hand, I will not put down my pumpkin for any reason. I cling to my pumpkin the way some pine trees clutch to the sides of cliffs. I'm rooted to it; it's an appendage now. There will be no putting it down for pictures or costume adjustments. When I have to scratch under my eye patch, I use the hook.

I'm eight and I've fallen in love with a swimsuit so rainbowed and vivid that it comes with its own tiny, plastic, banana-yellow sunglasses. My best friend, Marissa, and I have emerged from the dressing room.

"Suck it in or name it," says my mother.

I want this swimsuit like a last wish but something in me deflates, and when I look in the mirror again, I feel the first sharp stab of humiliation. The swimsuit is perfect. Two perfect oval windows cut out of the sides. But if you look through those windows there is a pinch of baby fat at my waist. The suit is ruined for me. Marissa bought one and wore it everyday, it seemed to me —clear into that Utah December—even to church. I bought a dreadful black maillot with a flouncy ruffled skirt thing to hide my little belly. The few times I went swimming were enough for me to learn how to shed layers—towel, and cover-up—so that, as I was jumping into the pool, my body was hitting the water's surface just as the airborne towel was suspended over the concrete edge and was close enough to be within reach as I pulled my body out of the water and into the towel upon finishing my self-conscious swim—so self-conscious, the pool might as well have been an aquarium. There was just one moment of pleasure: buoyed by water and suspended there, light at last and full of grace.

Here where the Puritan traditions still work to squelch pleasure both in the erotic and the gustatory, I give food a fond lover's attention. Even before I developed diabetes, I would dream not of Farrah Fawcett, chilly in a burnt orange swimsuit and smiling from her altar above my dresser, but of my mattress transformed into a huge rectangle of cheesecake. So when I consider my abiding love of food in relation to this affliction, I think of Beethoven without his hearing and Milton without his sight. The irony harkens back to fifth century Athens. This diabetes inspired my belief in Fate, a spiteful Fate. Still, I know full well that there are worse ailments to have. With this, at least, I won't be gaining any weight since weight gain is, technically, a healthy cellular response. The more I eat, the more my blood sugar fluctuates, the more weight I actually lose. The style of living that diabetes imposes is the difficulty. It requires balance, moderation, and control—three traits I do not possess in excess. It's a difficult balance to maintain, but balance, by definition, always is. It seems axiomatic that the more human nature is restrained, the worse it will be when it finally frees itself. When I finally tire of blandly wholesome fare, I binge like a jack monk in Vegas.

By nine I was drinking Fresca and Slim-Fast powdered lunch with skim milk, in the days before Nestle's Success Shake. I was nine years old and starting the first in a string of over 60 diets, all of which would fail. Instead they backfired with their quick-fix mentality. It would take me years to learn what now seems like common sense: motion and moderation. Dieting would take years and a toll on my physical health. But for all the time it took to get the fat off the girl, it would take twice as long to get the fat girl off my back. I used to make my own fat jokes. I may be fat, I reasoned, but at least I know I am. So I'd beat everyone to the punch line. Paunch line.

Sometimes, even now, when he says "you're beautiful," she's there again—the fat girl on my shoulder whispering cruel little contradictions. "Beautiful?" she says, "Surely, he means plentiful......"

There is a Success shake in the refrigerator right now. Chocolate. It almost went unnoticed there behind the fish sauce and jalapeño mustard. I know it is there, though; it's a food trophy, it's my mind's sore tooth.

Driving down the highway and I see the familiar bumper sticker. NO FAT CHICKS. Though she is over a decade behind me, she is there at these times—the fat girl I carry even now, sometimes, hot-faced and shameful, then enraged at that trucker. The three words mean to sting every woman who struggles on a daily basis to meet a harsh world's idea of thin enough, every woman who is unlucky enough to be caught behind the offensive vehicle, chrome, naked-silhouetted chick on the mud flaps and all. It always makes me angry. Funny thing how so many of those bumper-stickered drivers have backsides as wide as their trucks—funny how many of these truckers sport thunder thighs and Buddha bellies. And then there are the others. The men secure enough in themselves, in their idea of beauty, to have a deep and varied appreciation of form. The ones who like flesh and women with an appetite, a generosity of spirit, the passionate nature that generosity implies. "Who wants to hold a bag of coat hangers, after all," these men declare.

The subtext at every meal:
Her trying not to gain weight.
Him trying not to lose.

There must be a perfect amount of olive oil to use when I cook a meal—enough to keep my platelets slippery, but just under her daily amount of fat intake. The way the word pancreas now holds a small world of meaning—the frail organza of it, the tissue fear.

Maybe it makes things twice as complicated, this love-hate triangle with food. Or maybe it breeds a level of understanding, a middle ground between the feast and the fast you battle alone, together. The great meals that go double appreciated. The small courtesies we afford one another. The small blue packets of artificial sweetener we carry for each other's coffee.

Such necessary sugar, such goings on.
                    -Anne Sexton

This is us. Midnight—the check-floating hour—in the supermarket reveling in a full grocery cart. The sweet serenade of the floor polishing machine and a food orgy on wheels. This is no one-night stand in the frozen foods. This is beyond chocolate decadence and sugar-free angel food cake. This is lust.

A-S. Kartsonis' work has appeared in *Other Voices, Many Mountains Moving, Hayden's Ferry Review, Painted Bride Quarterly*, and *Walking the Twilight: An Anthology of Women Writers of the Southwest*. She is currently completing an M.F.A. degree while writing and teaching in Alabama.

Eliot Kahlil Wilson's work has appeared in *Beloit Poetry Journal, The Journal, Carolina Quarterly, Quarterly West, Persimmon Review,* and *Willow Spring*. He was a finalist in the Glimmer Train Poetry Open and the Academy of American Poets Prize. He has recently completed a Ph.D. at the University of Alabama where he served as an assistant fiction editor for the *Black Warrior Review*.

"Living the Sweet Life" was inspired by the realization that the idea of food and bodies are rarely neutral concepts for anyone, but in the case of a formerly overweight woman and a diabetic man, they are extra complicated. Food is both peril and sanctuary—more than an issue of sustenance. This essay is the result of our awareness of our dual bi-polar relationship to food—the way we continually swing between pious forbearance and backsliding abandon.

LIQUID AMBER

There is never a spring
I don't recall
glistening amber
of dandelion wine
when weeds, yellow-fringed
swaying over spiked salad greens
proliferate in grass,
nor ever a summer
I don't recall
the message of mystery
sent out with a puff
as gossamer seedlings
sail freely
with promise of dandelion wine
to come.

ROMANZA

"Never again," she told Paul as she finished scouring the last of the saucepans. "Never again. If you want fish, go out to eat. Go to Romanza."

"Romanza's been closed for weeks," he said. "You know that."

"And it's my fault? Take it out on me. Make me sick on the smell of your fish."

"Calamari," he said.

"Right. Italian fish."

"It's one meal. And it's not a fish," he said. "You're overreacting."

"I'm breathing, and it's making me sick."

"Let me finish the dishes," he said.

"I can manage," she said. "At least I can make sure there's nothing left to be smelling up the house. At least it'll be done right."

"I don't smell a thing."

She placed the short stack of wet Corningware on the small maple table. "You don't smell dead fish."

"It's not a fish..."

"I know. It's Calamari," she interrupted with an exaggerated Italian inflection. "Someone somewhere dragged it up out of the ocean. It's fish."

In all honesty, Paul could smell nothing. He could only revisit the taste he had experienced that evening, perhaps for the last time. Romanza was gone. Gone too was Antonio, the chef who had first described so lovingly to Paul his calamari with linguine in hot tomato sauce. The chef was to blame. Two years earlier Paul did not know calamari from cannoli. Although friends had raved over his talents in the kitchen, most of his experience with Italian cuisine had come from his visits to the takeout chain restaurant wedged between the Macys and Bloomingdales at the East 61 shopping complex. Or Angelo's Pizza, where he would stop in for an occasional slice and beer. But Romanza. Why had he ever visited the place? Why had his wife gone out of town and left him to dine alone? Why couldn't he have been satisfied microwaving a square of Gerard's frozen Sicilian? There was enough blame to go around, but finally, it was his own weakness and nothing more.

"Never again," she repeated.

Water dripped from the handles of pale blue coffee cups and the rims of saucers. With a damp towel Paul slid the dishes to one side and mopped up the pool that had formed beneath them. Madeline stacked dishes in silence, but her words echoed in Paul's head. "Never again. Never again."

Calamari. The delicate aroma of sea breeze, sand scrub, and salt air. The playful spray of blacks and violets over the firm flesh of squid. Never again. The tentacles, full and blooming like an exotic ocean flower. The eyes, small and clear. Never again.

He tried to entice her by describing the fragrance of the sauce— the blend of Roma tomatoes, garlic, basil, serrano peppers. He told her of the bed of linguine and the sprinkling of pecorino cheese. He described the explosion of the flavors as they swirled around his tongue, the anticipation of each passionate bite, the final act of swallowing.

She hated it. It was a hatred that transcended taste. He liked vanilla. She liked chocolate. That was that. But calamari was an imperfection as much as a meal; Paul had acquired a blemish that simply would not fade. When he ate it she would not kiss him or touch him or embrace him. She could not allow it to be part of her life, and as such, it could never be part of Paul's.

To forget the calamari, he would immerse himself in his work, a weekly political cartoon strip he drew for the local paper. But his strength as a cartoonist lay in his adroitness in quick observation more than his artistic or social insight, and he was usually finished by mid-morning. That left him time to be swallowed up by his obsession, especially when his wife was out of town at one of her frequent marketing conferences. When she was gone for longer than a few days, he would prepare enough sauce and slice enough calamari to carry him through to her return, eating it sometimes three or four days in a row.

More frequently, she would be gone for the weekend, and although he was happy to see her return, a single weekend was not enough time to prepare, consume, and clean up. The residual odor would remain. On these weekends, he would be satisfied to tour the market, touch the squid, and dream of the next encounter.

One weekend, when he had a particularly strong craving for calamari, and his wife was away overnight on business, he struck on a clever idea, one that, if successful, would enable him to enjoy his favorite food without his wife ever knowing. It occurred to him that while she had an acute sense of smell, one that rivaled any woman's he had ever known, calamari was not all that strong, and could possibly be masked by another, more telling odor. Imagine all the foods capable of overpowering calamari, he thought to himself. There was garlic. No. He would have to sauté an entire braid, and then what would he do with it. A curry, perhaps. No. His wife already knew that he hated East Indian cuisine and would wonder why he was spending his day preparing something he hated. He considered taking up pickling. He could buy bushel baskets of miniature gherkins. The kitchen would be bathed in the scents of dill and vinegar and garlic and peppercorns. No. He would need canning supplies—mason jars and lids and rubber rings, steam baths and tongs, thermometers—not to mention the extra shelving necessary to store the finished product. So many pickles.

Then he remembered. The Stegmanns: the family that had only recently moved into the neighborhood. In a conversation he had had with them shortly after their arrival, Carl Stegmann had mentioned their regret in having to sell their Amish homestead in central Pennsylvania. The one-time farmer now taught history at the local high school.

"Couldn't compete with the multiplexes anymore," Carl had told him. "People in Pennsylvania like movies better than they do fresh corn and tomatoes. They paid me more than the farming profits of a lifetime to sell," he said. "Couldn't turn it down, what with a growing family and my prices so low." He laughed. "Guess they're eating popcorn back home by now." His laughter fell flat.

They had lost other things to the farm: the quiet of night, the dark, the stars. When he pointed out to Paul the dim glimmer of Orion, while mistaking it for the Little Dipper, Carl explained how at night he and his wife would sit in the dining room next to the bow window, then turn out the track lighting and motion sensors to search the sky for the moon and stars lost in the glare of the bright suburban lights. Stars were what they missed most. There was also the lost Amish cuisine—the flavors of snitz and knepp, bratwurst and cabbage, Harvard beets, baked dried corn—all the fragrances and flavors that made their small farm a home. Amish cooking was a rare treat in their new suburban neighborhood.

Paul had some knowledge of their native region. He had driven through the heart of Amish country before. He had visited the recreated Pennsylvania Dutch homesteads. He had seen the replicas of the square, black buggies parked at the entrance to the Holiday Inn. He had followed the miles of billboards directing him to family-style restaurants, to the traditional seven sweets and seven sours. He had seen the glare of headlights from mounting tourist traffic as each night it clogged the narrow roads. Maybe he couldn't give them the stars, but he could give them back their culture. The decision was final. He would prepare the Stegmanns a feast, a smorgasbord of meats and vegetables and pastries—sausages cooked in yellow onions and green bell peppers, pork simmered in fresh sauerkraut and brown sugar, ham, apples, drop dumplings. And the shoo fly pie—wet and sweet with butter and sugar and molasses. The fragrances would be overwhelming and too varied to identify. Even with his wife's seasoned sense of smell, the odor of calamari would be impossible to distinguish among the rest.

The next evening, as he lay in bed with his wife, his arm gently encircling her, he pondered the scenario. Normally he would be eased into sleep by the wisp of his wife's breathing. Now, his eyes were wide open as she slept. A smile spread across his face, a smile that seemed enormous and would have taken some explaining if discovered. Outside, the street was unusually quiet. Moths tapped the floodlight outside the bedroom window. Cicadas sang from the lone tree in Mrs. Scott's front yard next door. An occasional cricket clicked against the vinyl sill beneath the outside screen. A warm breeze carried through the open window, and with it a serene dream of hot virgin olive oil and rings of soft sea flesh. Soothed by the night and comforted by his desire, he gently slipped into a late spring slumber.

The next morning they made love. Afterward, Madeline rolled next to him and lay against the curve of his chest.

"I've been thinking about Romanza," she said.

"What brought that on?"

"Your love for that awful food, I suppose," she said as she wrinkled her face. "Maybe you should be a chef instead of a cartoonist."

"That would be a mistake," he said.

"Why?" she asked. "Cooking seems to agree with you. Even if it is that horrible food."

"You've forgotten about my art already?" he asked.

"I love your little cartoons," she said.

"I mean my art," he said. "That little studio I used to have. How far into debt did that run us?"

"But it paid off," she said. "Would anyone have taken notice without it? Would you have landed your own strip without it?"

"What was it they noticed?" he replied. "Offbeat characters that might amuse some guy as he's having his morning coffee? Or some corporate manager on an afternoon commuter train? Can you imagine if I were a chef? I'd be marketing a line of frozen fish fillets by year's end."

"Everybody can't be a Picasso," she said as she twirled his hair.

"Exactly," he said. "Remember what happened to Romanza. That chef was an artist. And where is he? When art gets tangled up in business, it kills the passion. Or it kills you. It's not a good idea either way."

"Well, I think you're a great artist and you'd make a great chef," she said. She brushed back his hair, kissed him, then rolled out of bed.

After gathering up her briefcase, Madeline embraced Paul as he sat at the kitchen table, drinking his coffee and reading his cartoon panel in the morning paper. "I really do love your cartoons," she told him, and planted a kiss on the side of his neck.

After his wife's departure, Paul launched his plan. He started by shopping for all of the ingredients he would need for his neighbors' feast. He scoured the aisles of Guillaume's Market, selecting the finest hams and sausages. He poured through displays at Shea's for potatoes and onions and cabbage. And the spices—fresh peppercorns, mustard seed, cloves, cinnamon. He filled his basket with sacks of pastry flour and sugars—brown, white, powdered. He bought the largest jar of molasses he could find for the sweet, wet shoo fly pie. Then he set to work on his own dinner, which was a much simpler task. Although it seemed he had been away from it for ages, he knew the ingredients by heart.

That afternoon, after preparing his meal and setting out the platters brimming with sauce and seafood and semolina pasta, the memories of his distant infatuation came flooding back. He approached the food playfully at first, tenderly nibbling at the crisp covering, so as not to consume it too quickly. The desire to do just that was strong—to drown the squid with sauce and fill his mouth, then crush the rings in his ravenous bite. At least through the first serving, he resisted the temptation. The second he finished more quickly, swirling the last fork full of linguine into the pool of sauce, then devouring what remained with the heel of a baguette. When he had finished the last of it, he sat at the table, sipping water, and inhaling the lingering odor, satisfied only when every trace of its existence had vanished.

With newfound energy, he cleaned up any evidence of calamari that he could find; he checked the trash bin for telltale wrappings and the drain for stray tentacles or eyes. He then set about assembling the ingredients for the second meal. He scored the ham rind and spiked it with cloves and a scattering of mustard seed. Then he peeled and sliced potatoes and onions and green bell peppers—drained the sauerkraut that would soon form the sweet and sour bed for the hearty bratwurst.

After the food was cooked, he allowed it to linger on the stove top so that every inch of the kitchen soaked up the fragrances of Pennsylvania Dutch cuisine. Exotic traces of Italy gave way to the quaint vestiges of the heartland of America. As finicky as his wife was, she could not disparage the likes of seven sweets and seven sours, especially when it arose from a simple neighborly gesture intended to bring their community closer together.

Paul took down the stack of plasticware and placed each course into a separate container. The ham he left in the black enamel roasting pan and sealed it with a large sheet of aluminum foil. He placed the filled containers neatly into a large cardboard box and started off for the Stegmanns. The box was not light, and although their

37

house was only across the street, his struggle with its weight was sure to be witnessed by other neighbors, further testament to his kind and decent act.

Carl Stegmann seemed suitably surprised to see Paul standing at his front door. The family had already been living there for nearly six months, and Paul had only spoken to him twice during that time. In fact, he had already forgotten how tall and muscular Carl was; the sleeves of his white shirt were rolled up well past his elbows revealing well-defined veins and forearms, the result, no doubt, of years of work in the fields. What remained of his hair was fair, sandy, but made lighter by his sun-darkened complexion.

Instead of looking at Paul, Carl stared at the box, apparently mystified by its contents, before inviting him into the house. It was Mrs. Stegmann who finally ushered him in through the living room as she wiped her hands on a large striped apron that covered the skirt of her dress. She was a small woman, half Carl's size, which made them look awkward together. Her chestnut brown hair had been gathered up and stuffed into a white net, the kind he had seen the Mennonites at the farmer's market wearing. Judging from the size of the net, he imagined her hair to be voluminous. She greeted him with a smiling, wide face that appeared especially pale next to her husband's ruddy complexion.

"Come in," the wife said brightly. She brushed easily past her husband and cleared a path for Paul. "Let him in, Carl," she said.

She continued a patter of small talk while she led Paul into the kitchen, with Carl close behind. "My, what a large box you have there," she said. "Whatever could it be. Set it down here. What a large, heavy box," she continued.

She led him toward the kitchen table, a glass and chrome structure that Paul doubted had any connection to Amish decor. Nowhere in the house were there heavy woods or hand hewn furniture or ladder back chairs, just lots of metal and glass. Then, Paul thought, this was not an Amish homestead, and they were no longer Amish homesteaders and were as entitled to the comforts of modern society as anyone. He set the box on the table.

"What have you brought there?" the wife asked, as she began to pluck plastic containers from the box. Her smile widened with the appearance of each new container. "Carl. Look at this," she said. She opened the container of bratwurst, onions, and peppers, but replaced the cover before he had a chance to look for himself. "And corn," she said with the next selection. "How wonderful. Ham," she said. "Carl, there's a ham in here. My goodness."

Her expressions of delight seemed to go on endlessly, and Paul could not help but feel pleased with his neighborly gesture, even if it hadn't arisen from the noblest of intentions.

"This is kind of you," Carl said, in a stilted delivery. "Did you prepare this yourself? So much work and trouble," he said.

"I thought we should get to know each other better, being neighbors and all," Paul told them, not considering it a lie. He and his wife had often discussed the declining roles of communities in contemporary society. Once, it had been the subject of his cartoon. If they had had more time it would have been a priority for them. No, it was not a lie. "You probably don't know this about me, but I do quite a lot of cooking. Kind of a hobby of mine," he said. "I'm always ready to tackle something new. So, I thought why not share it as a gift."

Mrs. Stegmann continued to remove containers, increasingly amazed at what each new layer revealed. "This is so kind of you," she said. "You must join us tonight. And your wife, too. You must both join us."

Paul was flattered by her invitation, but he explained how his wife would be out of town for another day, and he would not think of intruding and would be fine on his own. Although they continued to insist, he resisted, explaining that they would be pleased to join them another time. He left them with their box of traditional food. Words of praise and appreciation followed him through the living room, and he walked home with a great sense of satisfaction. He had taken the first step toward reinforcing the idea of community in his corner of the world. Mostly, he thought about calamari.

"Have you been cooking?" Madeline asked when she returned from her business trip the following evening.

"Spinach soufflés. Frozen," he said, and pulled two dishes from the microwave. He set them on the table next to a foil tray of snow-flake rolls and a dish of butter.

"There's something else," she said. "I can't quite put my finger on it. Another odor."

"Oh that," he said, dismissing her comment out of hand. "I whipped up a little something for our new neighbors. You know. The farmers."

"Really? What made you decide to do that?"

"We're always talking about the vanishing community," he said. "Thought we should get to know them before they disappear."

He told Madeline about the multiplex cinema and the farm sale. He told her about the bratwurst, sauerkraut, and creamed corn. He told her about the glass and chrome furniture. He even told her about the invitation to join them for dinner one evening when it was convenient. She seemed genuinely impressed.

"You've been a busy man," she said playfully. She wrapped her arms around him and held him against the kitchen sink. She kissed the base of his neck. "My thoughtful, busy man," she said.

"It's no big deal."

"Just keep cooking," she whispered into his ear.

That night they made love.

At the end of the following week, the events repeated themselves. His wife gave him an equally affectionate farewell and left for another out-of-town business session. Like the last time, he went to the market and bought the ingredients for his Amish dinner.

And, just as he had done before, he selected the finest squid from the Italian market. His calamari only improved with practice. His fear that he might eventually grow tired of the dish diminished as his desire grew stronger.

Then, as he had done the previous week, he packed up a cardboard carton with the Amish meal and carried it across the street to his neighbors' house. Once again, he was greeted with surprise and joy at the sight of the prepared dinner. And, as he had done the last time, he swore to the Stegmanns that he and his wife would join them for dinner at their earliest convenience.

When he returned home, he reveled in the scent that filled his kitchen—vinegar, sugar, cloves—ever more pleased with himself over his incredible stroke of luck. While the Stegmanns longed for their old country home, his culinary future was secure. His wife's business project continued for the next several weeks, as did his routine of cooking, first for himself, then for the Stegmanns. Whenever the excitement over his visits appeared to be waning, he would change the menu—au-gratin potatoes rather than scalloped, cranberry relish rather than sweet and sour cabbage. So devoted was he to their happiness that he purchased a Pennsylvania Dutch primer on cooking techniques to spice up his menu.

One afternoon, after carrying the boxed dinner over to the Stegmanns' house, he was greeted at the door with the usual promptness, but this time by Mrs. Stegmann. Not knowing her first name, he continued to call her Mrs. Stegmann, even as he engaged in small talk with her. She was wearing her usual black and white dress, her striped apron, and her hair net. Her bright eyes followed his as he set the box on the kitchen table. As she began to lift out the plastic containers, he glanced around the kitchen and into the dinning room, but did not see Carl.

"This is so kind of you. More than you should be doing," Mrs. Stegmann said, with her normal tone of appreciation. "Won't you stay for supper?" she asked.

A genuine need appeared in her eyes that Paul had not seen before, and he found it difficult to resist. He could not tell if it was simply a need to return his kindness, or a genuine loneliness that had taken hold of her since his last visit. Either way, he felt uncomfortable.

"I really don't want to impose," Paul answered. "I'm not all that hungry right now anyway."

"But so much of this will only go to waste if you don't stay," she pleaded. "Carl and the children are staying with his mother for a few days, and I'll be eating alone. Would be a sin to see all your efforts spent on just one person."

Despite his well intentioned discussions with Madeline, Paul had never planned on becoming close to any of his neighbors, least of all the family of farmers across the street, but there was a pathetic quality in her voice that touched him. They had done him a larger favor then they would ever know. He had good reason to return it.

"I'd be happy to stay," he said.

Over and over, she thanked him. She placed her hand on his. The skin of her small palm was rough and warm. She continued to thank him as she placed the food in the refrigerator. Then she placed her hand along his cheek. Now, her hand felt softer, but cold. He told her that he needed to take care of some things and that he would return in an hour. She escorted him to the door, and he rushed across the street to his own house.

Once inside, he cleaned the dishes and pots and pans he had used for cooking that day. As he had become accustomed to doing, he checked the entire kitchen for any remains of squid or overlooked wrappings. When he was satisfied, he showered and dressed. Certain that everything had been taken care of, he returned to Mrs. Stegmann's house. She too had dressed for dinner, which he recognized not so much by any marked change in fashion, but by the fresh apron tied around her waste—a pastel green and yellow. The hair beneath her net had been rewrapped. She invited him into the house, offering the same gentle touch on his arm with which he had departed earlier.

The glass and chrome table in the kitchen had already been set. Two white ironstone dinner plates sat on place mats accented with a green gingham print. In the center of the table stood bowls that had been filled with the food Paul had brought over earlier. While he might have normally felt uncomfortable at the table of a new acquaintance, his familiarity with the corn and the potatoes, the relish and sausage made him feel instantly at ease, as if they were old friends come to join them. As they ate, Mrs. Stegmann talked about her family—Carl's classes at the local high school, their awkward adjustment to the suburbs, friends they had made in the neighborhood.

"Carl misses the farm," she told him. "It was the world to him."

"City life must take getting used to."

"I suppose. But it's easier for me and the children than for Carl."

"Tough changing what you are," Paul said. "When you're a farmer, you're a farmer." He cringed at his trite comment. Work for him was drawing forgettable stick figures. What did he know about farming? What did he know about commitment?

"For some, I suppose," she said. "Least while, the day's shorter teaching. How bad can it be not having to work from sunup to sundown every day?"

"Still, it can't be easy for him," he said.

She traced her finger around the rim of the water glass. "Practically had to drag him from the county clerk's office. Had a hard time letting it go."

"What about you?" he asked. "Isn't this all new to you?"

"I guess I adapt a little more quickly." She ran her palm along the edge of the glass table top.

"Pretty simple there, though, that farm life," he said.

She clutched the glass top. "Simple," she said. "Can't get much simpler than open fields and corn rows. Is that what you think?

Even simpler watching it through farmhouse windows and canning jars." She filled Paul's glass with water, then wiped away the ring of moisture before setting down the pitcher. "But how many things in this world can you bear never changing?" she said.

"Guess I always thought of farm life as pure... less complex," he said.

She smiled. "They don't have cartoonists and chefs where I come from. If that's what you consider less complex, I guess you're right."

She was amused, she explained, at the notion that something like drawing cartoons would actually be someone's profession, but Paul was accustomed to such a reaction and joked with her about it as he helped himself to another serving of baked corn.

"Show me your cartoons," Mrs. Stegmann said suddenly.

Paul placed his fork, already halfway to his mouth, back on his plate. Beneath the table, he stroked the fabric of his napkin between his thumb and forefinger. Mrs. Stegmann, her gaze lowered, pushed her remaining dinner from one side of her plate to the other.

"Why?" he asked.

"I've never met an artist before," she said without looking up.

"I'm seldom referred to as an artist," he replied as he stared at her and continued to rub his wrinkled napkin. "I'm afraid you'd be disappointed."

She raised her blushing face and said, "Your cooking's artistic. This is the first time I've tasted it, but I've smelled it before."

He lay his napkin beside his plate. "My food?" he asked, surprised by her admission.

"Only one odor, really," she said. "I can only smell it when I'm in the yard, but it's always the same odor."

"Are you certain it's from my house?" he asked, trying to remain calm by piercing a chunk of summer sausage.

"I wasn't sure... until I followed the aroma one day," she said quietly. "Terrible of me, I know, but it was such a heavenly aroma."

Paul's fingers pressed the length of the fold in the napkin. "If you describe it, I can probably tell you what it is," he said.

She began to describe what he had feared, the scent of calamari with linguine in hot tomato sauce. She described it perfectly for someone not familiar with Italian food—tomato, garlic, peppers, cheese, all wafting through the street on a sweet ocean breeze. So perfect was her description that it conjured images of the dish, and he found his attention drifting from his original question, away from discussions of art and Pennsylvania, away from bratwurst and pickled relish.

"Do you recognize that?" she asked. She playfully patted his hand.

"Yes," he said, too dazed by his neighbor's revelation to notice her fingers on his.

"Could you do something for me?" she asked.

"What?" he said.

"Would you make that for me?" she asked. Her face flushed red, and she smiled.

"Sure," he replied without thinking. "Tomorrow?"

"That would be wonderful," she told him.

He felt her hand brush lightly over the back of his, but then his senses began to fade, and he could see nothing but the wheat wall in the dining room. Everything else disappeared. Somewhere in the back of his mind he heard the clatter of ironstone. When he was finally able to move his eyes, he saw Mrs. Stegmann, still talking over the sound of the running water as it splashed away the remains of cabbage and potatoes. She smiled, then rinsed.

The next morning, Paul went through his normal routine of shopping and browsing and selecting. At home he prepared the calamari. It seemed that he had done it so often that he scarcely had to think about it anymore. Only this time, instead of savoring the meal himself, he began packing it into the stack of plastic containers that had previously held Amish fare. He was freely offering his passion to another woman, something he was certain he would never do.

As he had done so often, he carried the box to the Stegmanns' front door. When it opened, the flimsy box nearly slipped from his hand. In the doorway stood Carl.

"Good afternoon, Paul," Carl said, smiling more broadly than usual. Before Paul thought of a reply, Mrs. Stegmann appeared behind her husband.

"Come in," she said as she led him into the kitchen. She spoke nervously as she lifted the box from his hands. "What luck Carl decided to come home early," she continued, as she began to remove the collection of containers.

"Dinner," Paul said, picking up on Mrs. Stegmann's unease. "I thought you'd like something different."

Carl peered into the box, his eyes focused and determined as he squinted at the plastic dishes. Paul thought he saw Carl's nose twitching, like a cat cautiously sniffing the air.

"Seafood," Paul quickly volunteered. "You must get tired of those land animals now and then." He laughed. "Isn't that right?" he said, slapping Carl on his broad back as he laughed once again. Carl looked bewildered.

"Never ate fish before," Carl said. He placed his hand on Mrs. Stegmann's shoulder, as if to include her in his comment.

"Never had much time to fish on the farm," she smiled.

"You'd be surprised what they farm nowadays," Paul said weakly as he watched the dish of calamari emerge from the box. Like many times before, Mrs. Stegmann invited him to stay for dinner. She set the tub of linguine next to the calamari, then the dish of sauce on top of it. Absently, he licked his bottom lip as he stared at the combination. He followed the sauce's descent onto the lower rack of the refrigerator and watched as the door swung close. Certainly there was some goodness in his neighborly gesture toward the Stegmanns. He was not that shallow a man. Everybody said so. But never had he intended to be so generous. Brazenly, Mrs. Stegmann touched his arm.

"Please. Stay," she said.

"No," he whispered, shaking his head. His head continued to shake as Carl led him to the front door, and as he crossed the street, and as he lifted and inserted the key into his own door. The scent of calamari hit him as he entered the kitchen and snapped him back into reality.

He immediately took steps to eliminate the scent of squid by preparing a full course Amish meal—seven sweets and seven sours. He cut potatoes and onions and peppers. He sautéed the knockwurst and creamed the corn, all as he had done before. But this time, the joy of the process had faded. The reasons for his work had changed. It was no longer the consequence of his own passion, but of his neighbors'. He simply went through the motions. After the meal was completed he sat at the table, set with a simple plate, a fork and a knife, and ate. He ate it all, blindly, not remembering the flavors or the textures of the corn or potatoes, not conscious of the act of biting and chewing and swallowing the lengths of sausage. The kitchen smelled pungent, like vinegar.

As he washed the dinner dishes, he stared through the window to the Stegmanns' house. Through their dining room window, he could see the place settings around the table, and the filled serving dishes in the center. He watched Mrs. Stegmann line each plate with a bed of linguine, as if it were second nature to her. He followed her hands as they spooned the calamari, then hot sauce over it. He thought he saw Carl smile.

When his wife arrived home that evening, he was already in bed. Although he was not sleeping, he lay there as if he were. He heard her come into the room. He listened as she quietly undressed. She crawled into bed, curling up against his back. Her arm circled around his waist. She wanted to make love. He could tell. If he had had the strength, they might have. He continued to breath as if sleeping.

The next morning, after Madeline was ready for work, she wrapped her arm around him, and left a moist kiss on his neck. He patted her hand and drank his coffee. When she left, he drew his stick figure frame and wrote his caption beneath it, but he did not think it was very witty.

In the afternoon, he ran into Mrs. Stegmann, who raved about how delicious the dinner was, how even Carl, who had never eaten any animal without hooves, talked about it all night. She thanked him and rethanked him, gave him a peck of fresh peaches that she had gotten from the market, and asked if he would be so kind as to prepare it for them again. Perhaps he and his wife could join them. He agreed to make the calamari, but again made an excuse for not joining them.

Over the course of the next few weeks, he shopped, chopped and cooked. He delivered calamari and ate German sausage. From his kitchen window, he watched the smiles on the faces of the Stegmanns as they filled their plates with his delicious food. He was amazed at how well they were adapting to life in the suburbs.

Each night when his wife came home he would lie in bed, breathing deeply, as if in a sound sleep. She would undress and lie beside him, but he would only breathe until she grew tired, turned over, and fell asleep. Only then could he finally doze off himself. One night she whispered into his ear.

"Has my cook been working too hard?"

"Umm. Could be. Night."

She ran her fingers across his cheek. "You should take some time out to shave anyway," she whispered. "It's okay though. I like your rugged side."

"I'll shave tomorrow. Good night."

After feeling Madeline settle onto her side, he fell asleep.

He missed his deadline. No stick figure. No clever caption. It seemed he was running out of them as quickly as his energy. He left the house only to pick up the paper from his front step in the morning, then shop in the afternoon. Sometimes, he would crawl back into bed, the paper covering him, but he never really read it. His beard was thick. His stomach was beginning to bulge from creamed potatoes and lying in bed. Occasionally he heard a knock at his front door, but he didn't answer.

One day, there was a more forceful knock on the door, a knock that persisted though Paul tried to ignore it. He tossed back his covers, wandered through the living room, and cracked open the door. On the stoop stood Carl Stegmann. He wore his usual white cotton shirt with the sleeves rolled up past his muscular forearms. He stood stiffly, and his eyes shifted to the small opening in the door.

"Morning, Carl," Paul murmured as he opened the door a few more inches.

"May I come in?" Carl asked abruptly.

"Sure ... sure." Paul opened the door and awkwardly waved his neighbor into the house. "Excuse the place. Sleeping in this morning. Coffee?"

"I won't keep you long," Carl said. "It's about your cooking."

Paul rubbed his bleary eyes. "Of course. Haven't even started yet. What time is it? Eleven o'clock? Should get going."

"That won't be necessary," he said. "Not that we don't appreciate your thoughtfulness. All the work you've gone through."

"What's the problem?" he said. "Calamari not up to par?"

"Calamari is the problem," he said. "I'm not one to be thinking ill of any man's efforts," he continued, "but there's something strange about all this food. I'm not saying you have any motives, but I prefer to raise my family among simple flavors. As for Mrs. Stegmann, she can scarcely taste sweets or sours anymore. Calamari. It's all she talks about."

"If you're suggesting..."

"I'm not suggesting anything except that you keep your food to yourself," he said. "Meat, potatoes, vegetables. They've always been good enough for us. That's the way I want to keep it."

"But I saw you eating," Paul said. "I saw you smiling."

"I suggest you keep your eyes and your food on your own table, and not on mine." He flexed his grip then released it. Without saying another word, he turned and stood facing the door until Paul opened it. He walked out and crossed the street with an unflinching stride. Paul scratched his unshaven chin as he walked to the kitchen window and watched his neighbor's door close. The blinds to the dining room lowered.

In the bathroom mirror, there was no longer any reflection of the cunning gourmet of a few weeks earlier. Then, he was happily a slave to his passion. With that passion disintegrating before his eyes, he was slave to nothing but his own vague memories. He thought of shaving. He thought of taking a shower and dressing. He thought of working on his cartoon panel. A brief recollection of the fragrance of calamari brought to mind the idea of eating, but he could not find the energy for any of it. In his bed, he pulled the covers up to his stubbled neck and closed his eyes. Dreams of lightly breaded sea rings were replaced by the residue of sugar and vinegar on his tongue. Only the rumble rising from his stomach brought back thoughts of Romanza. Romanza. He cursed the word.

On the morning that Madeline left him, she was sobbing as he lay curled beneath the covers. She told him that she could no longer accept the changes in him. Through her tears, she asked him the questions that he would have expected her to ask—what had happened to him, why would he no longer touch her, why had he lost his passion for living, for her? But he did not dare tell her about the Stegmanns, about the calamari, so he sighed and said nothing.

One day, as Paul was lying in bed, browsing through the help wanted ads, he took notice of a small advertisement at the bottom of page D3. "Romanza II," it read. "Chef Antonio Gilbrati is pleased to announce the opening of his new restaurant at the corner of Third and Albright. He is pleased to be serving the community once again with fine Italian cuisine." At the bottom of the ad, in Roman italics it read, *"Our specialty—Calamari."*

Months passed before Paul finally found the will or the energy to visit Antonio's new restaurant. He sat at a small, dark booth, in the back of the dining area. He glanced over the menu, as if genuinely interested in all they had to offer, though he knew he would remain faithful to the calamari. As he sipped on his glass of house wine, he observed diners twirling pasta and swallowing mussels.

Across the room at a small table sat a man and a woman who were drinking red wine, talking, laughing. Only after staring at the woman for some time did he finally recognize her as Madeline. He had never seen the man before, a young, dark man, with jet black hair. When he spoke to her, she laughed in the same way she had laughed at Paul's conversation when they first met. In a moment of silence, she shyly look away, then turned back as the man lifted his fork from his plate and held it out toward her. Entwined in the tines of the fork was a ring of calamari. Madeline hesitated, then slowly moved forward. Her lips wrapped around the fork. She drew it into her smile.

The lights throughout the parking lot were mostly out, and the walkway leading to Paul's car was thrown into unexpected darkness. A sign at the end of the sidewalk, illuminated by a single bare bulb read, "THE MANAGEMENT APOLOGIZES FOR THE IN-CONVENIENCE—WATCH YOUR STEP." The moon was merely a crescent, but when Paul traced its curve toward the horizon, he could clearly make out each glimmering point of Orion. There was no mistaking it for the Little Dipper. As he drove toward the exit, his eyes followed the cluster of stars. On the main road they dimmed, and were finally lost in the glare of the suburban lights.

Jeffrey Ihlenfeldt has an MFA from Goddard College and presently teaches writing at Mercer County Community College in Trenton, New Jersey and Community College of Philadelphia in Pennsylvania. His stories have appeared in a number of publications including *Southern Humanities Review, Farmer's Market, Owen Wister Review,* and *City Primeval.*

"'Romanza'— Suburban mythology, if such a thing exists, is steeped in an environment of chain restaurants, fast food, and frozen entrees. And it is in just such an environment that passion is forced to survive...or not. I set out to explore the intimate relationship of one man and one woman in one neighborhood, but wound up discovering a 'suburban myth' of operatic proportions."

Beth Ann Fennelly

WHY I CAN'T COOK FOR YOUR SELF-CENTERED ARCHITECT COUSIN

Because to me a dinner table's like a bed—
without love, it's all appetite and stains. Let's buy
take-out for your cousin, or order pizza—his toppings—

but I can't lift my spatula to serve him what I am.
Instead, invite our favorite misfits over: I'll feed
shaggy Otis who, after filet mignon, raised his plate

and sipped merlot sauce with such pleasure
my ego pardoned his manners. Or I'll call Melody,
the chubby librarian, who paused over tiramisu—

"I haven't felt so loved since. . ." then cried into its curls
of chocolate. Or perhaps neurotic Randolf will appear,
who once, celebrating his breakup with the vegetarian,

so packed the purse seine of his wiry body with shrimp
he unbuttoned his corduroys and spent the evening
couched, "waiting for the swelling to go down."

Or maybe I'll just cook for us. I'll crush the pine nuts
unhinged from the cones' prickly shingles.
I'll whittle the parmesan, and if I grate a knuckle

it's just more of me in my cooking. I'll disrobe
garlic cloves of their rosy sheaths, thresh the basil
till moist, and liberate the oil. Then I'll dance

that green joy through the fettucine, a tumbling,
leggy dish we'll imitate, after dessert.
If my embrace detects the five pounds you win

each year, you will merely seem a generous
portion. And if you bring my hand to your lips
and smell the garlic that lingers, that scents

the sweat you lick from the hollows of my clavicles,
you're tasting the reason that I can't cook
for your cousin—my strongly seasoned love.

WAITING

"You ever spit in anybody's food?" Pearl asked David. She reached for a bowl of salsa.

"For crying out loud, Pearl." David yanked a chip away from his mouth and examined it.

"I didn't mean I'd spit in *your* food," she said. "I meant, you know," she waved in the general direction of the few late diners. "Them."

David and Pearl sat at the bar. There were two couples and one four-top nursing coffee and drinks. Except for the kitchen crew cleaning up, they were the only ones in the restaurant at the end of a busy Saturday night.

"Last summer when they were filming that movie," Pearl began.

"The one with Cher?" David glanced over at his tables to see if anyone was getting ready to leave.

"That crew, they were such assholes. Not the big guys that actually did the work. They weren't bad. It was those toads who thought they were hot stuff, just because they were in the movie business." She scooped another chip and dripped salsa on the bar. "Their jobs were to do whatever people told them to do. They waited on people. Same as us. So they come in here, four o'clock in the afternoon and they want breakfast. All day, everybody ordering them around, so now its their turn to order *me* around. 'We don't serve breakfast now,' I tell them. But this one guy, he turns around and says real smarmy, 'Oh, I'm sure you can do something about that for us.' And he hands me the menus. Like it's already decided. Yeah, right, there *is* something I can do about that."

"So you spit in their food?"

"No, just their coffee. But not into each individual cup. I wasn't motivated enough to go to that much trouble, so I just spit in the coffee pot a few times." She smeared a French fry through a puddle of mayonnaise. "Just in case they didn't drink coffee, I licked some of their ice cubes, too."

Ricky from the kitchen put a plate in the window.

"My wings are up. Could you get them?"

David got up and went behind the bar to the service window. He placed a plate of chicken wings and bleu cheese dip in front of Pearl. She plucked a chicken wing out of the pile with two fingers and dragged it through the dip, leaving an oily orange trail.

"Thanks. Have some." The hot sauce made her lips tingle.

"Ah, geez," David said. He was looking past Pearl to the front entrance.

"What?" She knew it couldn't be Manny, the owner. He would come in through the kitchen. She turned in her seat and saw it was Rick, her ex-boyfriend.

"I'm going to clean up these tables," David said. The customers were starting to get up and leave, and David grabbed a tray for the glasses and cups.

Rick carefully stepped up to the bar and pulled a stool out. He sat down, leaving one empty seat between him and Pearl. He was wearing a denim shirt, jeans and heavy work boots. He put his hands on the bar and curled his fingers as if around an imaginary beer bottle. His hands were callused with dark scars.

"What's up?" Pearl asked. She slid off her stool and went behind the bar. She popped open a Rolling Rock and placed it in front of him, no glass. She thought he looked a little stoned.

Rick took the bottle and tipped it to his mouth. Pearl watched his Adam's apple bob three times.

"You getting out soon?" He licked beer from his mouth.

"Why?" It was hard for her to look at him. It was only a month ago he told her he wanted to break up with her so he could see other people. He had caused her too much heartache, but right then she felt like touching his fingers. She wanted him to take her in his arms and hold her. She wanted him to tell her he'd quit smoking pot, for real, and he'd get a job, and he'd pay her the rest of the money he owed her. And he'd be nice to her. He could be so nice, sometimes.

"Feel like going for a ride?" He tilted the bottle to his lips again.

"I don't know." Pearl looked at David, who was coming behind the bar with a tray full of glasses.

"You okay?" David asked Pearl. He glared at Rick. "What happen, lose your license again?"

"Everything is okay," Pearl said. "We're just going for a ride."

"Oh, for crying out loud, Pearl," David said, as if Rick couldn't hear him. "The guy is such a loser."

"It's just a ride," Pearl said, and she began to clear away their dishes from the bar.

"Just a ride," Rick said, smiling at David. He emptied the bottle with two more swallows. "I'll meet you outside."

"Hey, wait a minute. You didn't pay for that," David said as Rick walked away.

"I never ordered anything. She just gave it to me." He smirked and left.

"Mind your own business," Pearl said when he was gone.

"Fine. Do what you have to do." David counted the money in his apron pocket and tossed some bills on the counter, Pearl's share of the tips he made. He turned and walked through the swinging door to the kitchen.

Pearl heard him punch out at the time clock and then slam the back door.

It's just a ride, she thought. What's his problem?

Pearl unlocked the car door from the inside, and Rick folded himself into the Chevette. She almost forgot how tall he was.

"Head up by the train station," he said as he slid the seat back all the way. His knees pressed against the glove compartment. "I want to show you something." A light rain was beginning to spatter the windshield. He put his seat belt on before she reminded him.

They were quiet as she drove. She didn't turn on the radio or ask him any questions. At the top of the hill, she stopped for a red light. Rain drummed impatient fingers on the car roof. She was nervous, and when the light changed to green, she almost stalled letting the clutch out too fast. She expected Rick to criticize her clumsy shifting, but he was just looking out the window.

"Go straight here?" she asked.

"Go forward, not straight," he said and grinned.

He *was* stoned, she thought. What an idiot.

"Right up here." Rick pointed to a road that led to a warehouse where she knew some of his friends partied. She had gone once — kegs of beer, pot, and half-raw hamburgers on a smoky grill.

"Look at this," he said as they pulled up to the building. "The apple blossoms are out. Isn't that pretty?"

The headlights illuminated the wild looking little tree. The white blossoms were brilliant against the black sky. Rick got out of the car and walked up to the tree. Spots of rain darkened his shirt. He broke off a few small branches and cradled them in his arms. He turned to wave, and smiled proudly. Pearl smiled back, even though she knew he couldn't see her in the car above the glare of the headlights. He looks so sweet, she thought. If only David could see him through her eyes. He'd understand.

Rick pulled open the passenger door and dumped the flowers onto the seat.

"Thanks for the ride." He slammed the door and ran towards

the warehouse.

Pearl watched him go, her mouth open, but no sound coming out. She looked at the seat next to her. The apple blossoms looked like pursed lips, unkissed, and smelled like decaying fruit.

"That fucking asshole."

Donna Childs lives and writes in a seaside town in Massachusetts with her handsome husband, Peter. She works as a librarian in Young Adult Services, and leads writing workshops for teenagers. She has had several short stories published in national magazines, and is working on a novel.

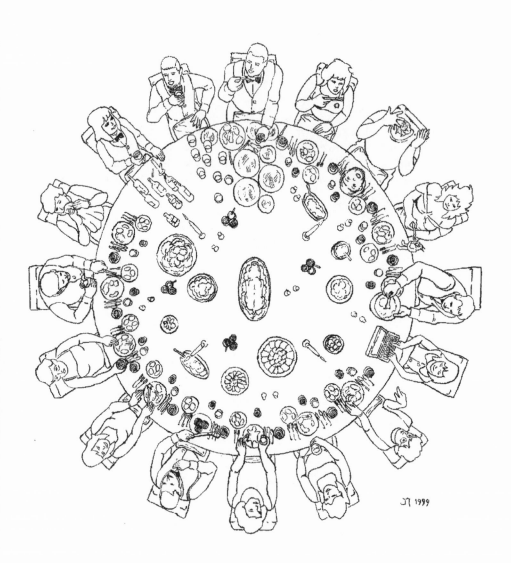

TWO HUNTERS' TALES

My brother lived in an imposing house. It was in New Jersey, one of many like it on a stretch of the old Post Road that ran from New York to Philadelphia. Out front his lawn was a wide clean sweep of close cropped grass, and along one side thick old trees, twisted with age, lined his driveway. It was a red brick house of the Georgian period, two stories high and formal, like most of the old houses there. This was a Tory town, and the house, like the town, had weathered insurrections, war and the slow flow of wealth which had accumulated there, money massing like snow, over time a glacier groaning under its own weight, moving mountains, etching valleys. Trees arched over the roads, shading them in the summer, littering them with a mad tangle of orange and yellow leaves in the fall, an archway small and muffled when the snows fell in winter.

His dining room was painted a dark hunter green, and the wood beams and chair rails around the room were stained dark, almost black. It was a room that felt rich when I found myself there, as I did once a year during Christmas, and maybe once or twice at other times during the year, when our parents were still healthy, and retired, and my brother was too busy to get back to Ice's Crossing, he was happy to have them back for a visit. When they came to New Jersey, my brother would ask me to come down from New England as well, thus killing two birds with the one visit in a house big enough for us all.

So it was one Christmas I was there, sitting at their long, oval table in a dark green room with paintings of hunters and hounds on every wall. His children sat next to me, one on each side. My niece wore a red velvet Christmas dress that belied her tomboy nature. My nephew wore a white shirt and a tie, and was quiet and self absorbed, as if he were plotting his escape from this contingent of strangers. My father was there across from me. I know now he had ten more years to live, but he had ceded much to my brother already, and my father often seemed uncomfortable, out of place, in New Jersey, or anywhere in fact other than his chair in front of the television set in their house in Ice's Crossing. My mother here had tucked a napkin in the collar of his shirt, as he never did anywhere else, a napkin such as he never otherwise put on, but here he let her tuck it in, no help from him but no struggle. He was an old and helpless tourist in my brother's foreign country. My mother sat next to him. With a nervous flutter of his fingers and with a word, he asked my mother to pass him the salt.

"Are we having coffee?" he asked, searching among his silverware and water glass for his cup. He salted all his food before he tasted it.

"We have coffee after meals, not before," my mother said. "They don't drink coffee with their meals in New Jersey."

My father did not say much as he explored the food in front of him, pushing it apart and back and forth, as if to see just what it was, where it started and where it stopped, passing judgment without saying a word. All this New Jersey stuff was new to him, and it confused him, the meal, the house, the manners, the richness of it. He felt tentative about it, unsure, cautious, not wanting to embarrass himself in the unfamiliar world in which his son now lived. Such wealth. For all his dreams, my father was not rich, not even close, and now retired and beyond much hope of achieving it, wealth in others made him uncomfortable, the formality of it. He could never be at ease, not in New Jersey, as was my brother, who had smoked the quails and now dished them out, one little quail to each to start.

"Do you like our dining room?" my brother asked. He sat at the head of the table. He wore a corduroy coat, which seemed casual and fitting, and his old lizard skin boots which he loved, he said, but never wore except when family was there. "Do you like the way we remodeled it?" He was broad shouldered, and in those days he always spoke with a smile. "Do you like the color?"

"I never seen a green dining room," my father said. He was trying to eat his peas with a fork but most of the peas ran off.

"I like it," my mother added quickly. "I love the color. It's nice to have such a big formal dining room," she added. "I know it's the way you do things back East. It's lovely."

My brother's wife sat the other end. There was food and silver on the table, candles and a red runner that stretched its whole length, all in a quiet, deep, wood-warm feel of Christmas. "We were happy we got it done in time for your visit."

We ate quail. These were little birds I had eaten only once before in all my life. They seemed then, as before, so little worth the effort, plucked and gutted and cooked down so one could fit in the curve of a spoon. They were tough little birds, and bony, and I picked at one, picking off the meat, tasting it, not much caring for their wild game taste. A dozen of these little birds would not quite make up for the meat in a single breast of turkey.

"You got these hunting?" I asked.

"Yeah," my brother said. "Last fall. Hunting up here, down in a south part of Jersey."

"I didn't know they had quail to hunt back here," I said.

"And pheasant. We got some pheasant, too," my brother said. "But we had the pheasant for dinner earlier this year. Dad hasn't had quail for twenty years, have you?" he asked. "So we're eating them at his request."

"Be careful, now," his wife said. "There's these little BB's in there."

There were indeed. I crunched into one, hoping the metal I felt in my mouth was a shot and not a filling. With my tongue rubbing against the roof of my mouth, I separated the shot from the meat and rolled it out to my lips where I grabbed with my thumb and finger and looked at it. "That's shot," I said. I showed it around the table.

"Yeah," my brother said. "There's a lot of those. We'll all find them."

I put it on the side of my plate, and threaded my way carefully through the bird, pulling it apart with knife and fork, and finding shot, both in the bird as I cut it and in the meat which I slowly, carefully chewed. My father had wrestled his quail around his plate, turning it and turning it as his fork tried to give his knife a purchase with which to cut, but the bird would turn and slide and his knife would click against my sister-in-law's fine Christmas china, scenes out of Dickens in red and green.

"Be careful, dear," my mother said, reaching over and taking my father's knife and fork. "There's buckshot in the meat." Without invitation, without resistance, she pulled and cut his bird apart as he leaned back in his chair and waited, the napkin stretching from his neck to his lap.

I liked my brother's house. I could not imagine anyone living here, or growing up here, letting it go, selling it, losing it. This was an old Tory town, but still it had a history and a dignity of time and care, as if it sat in the very center of the hub of all the seasons. The wood was thick in the floors and the stairs, the plaster cool and deep. A fire was kept going all winter in the fireplace downstairs, and although it did not heat the house nearly as well as it drew in a cold draught from outside, it was warm when you stood close to the fire, and it had a delightful glow that filled a room, even as it was dying. It was a great pleasure to sit in my brother's living room in the deep of winter in some deep-cushioned chair, lap up the glow of fire, and let a rich dinner course through the blood, nodding, and listening and unafraid, maybe reading a book, maybe nodding off like some old dying ember. The television was often on before dinner and after, and no one talked much.

For all the different ways that we had gone in our lives—and my brother and I had gone quite different ways—I felt we had something in common. Not method, nor approach, nor ways of being, or talking, nor even a theory of the nature of man. Those we differed on. But deeper than all of that, both of us were driven, as if by an inner hunger, one that had flung us out of Kansas, a yearning, maybe an emptiness. It could have been the place, Kansas, Ice's Crossing, or it could have been some odd assortment of the genetics of him and her that had conspired to make us so uncomfortable with ourselves. It could have been the water. Whatever it was, I felt driven, and he was driven, too. That was our bond.

"They don't have pheasant back here," my father said. He talked while he ate, absorbed in the act of eating. "They get these pheasants from where, North Carolina, and they bring them up here so guys can hunt. What'd they do?" he asked, turning to my brother. "Remember?" he asked. "Remember you told me?" then he turned to tell the rest of us at the table the story as if my brother was not there at all. "He wondered why they had all these kids coming out with them on the hunt, out so early in the morning. Five or six o'clock. He was out there with four or five guys, right?, and these kids that worked at this place all took off while they were having a drink. Can't go hunting without drinking. Not back here. So, later, when your brother," he said to me, "and his friends were out walking in the field. What was it? Scrub pine except for this place which was near the ocean, grass and scrubs, like Kansas, I suppose, imagine that. And then your brother hears these kids. And the guide who has taken them out that morning, he says, 'Boys, get your guns ready,' and there they were, your brother said, these kids about a hundred yards away…"

I just nodded to him and picked at the quail with my fork.

"Two hundred away," my brother said. "And they weren't kids. They worked there. They were guys. They called them beaters."

"…or so, and kicking the grass, and beating the grass, and the sun was just coming up, your brother said, and it was a perfect day, wasn't it, didn't you say?"

My brother nodded. He poured more wine and, with his eyebrows raised for my nod, topped off my glass as well. Our parents did not drink wine. His wife at the other end of the table was worried about his drinking.

"Ready for what? he wondered," my father continued. "And then the birds flew up. The kids were out there chasing them up, the beaters, quails and pheasants and whatever else was hiding in the grass. These kids, the beaters, they sent them out while these guys were still having their drinks, sent them out to the end of the fields. See, what this place did was, they brought these quail and pheasants in the day before. They raise these things in North Carolina…."

"Actually South Carolina."

"They truck them up to New Jersey. The night before the hunt they take them out to the field and let them go. Don't let them go too early." He was holding one leg of the quail in a hand. He bit down on it, then pulled the bone out, stripped of meat, and he continued talking while he chewed. He looked at what remained of the quail, a loose conglomeration now of bones and meat. "Too early and the damned things would be on their way back to North Carolina. Of course, the damned birds already had to be scared to death," he said, and he reached in his mouth and retrieved a small round shot that he had worked to his lips with his tongue. "A dog wouldn't be much good. A dog couldn't flush them out. A dog wouldn't hardly get the scent of birds that had only been there for an hour or two, I'd think. Paying what these guys paid, how much did you pay? a lot, anyway, you wouldn't want to spend a half a day and see just three or four pheasants, now would you, so these guys, the beaters, 'd scare up a bunch of birds…."

"It's dinner, sweetheart," mother said.

".....scared to death and they come flying right at these guys, a hundred birds or so, right?"

"A lot."

"I'd say. Flying right at you. Delivered. The damnedest thing. And these guys, half crocked, start shooting, my god, of course you'd get your limit if there's any limit on a private deal like that...."

"No limit," my brother said calmly. He was leaning back, smiling, listening to my father tell his story. "All you can shoot. All you want to shoot. It's by-the-hour."

"How can you fail, I'd say, unless you call it sport."

The peas almost rolled off my own fork. The pictures on the wall had caught my eye. They were a series on the sporting life—dogs, the fields, the guns, and beautiful pheasants dead on the ground. What was sport, then, but some carefully preserved part of the savage.

"Those look like the prints that grandpa used to have," I said. "Down on the old place."

"They are," my brother said. "I bought them. Just like them. Had them framed. I'm buying back the farm as well," he announced.

"What farm?" I asked. "Our old place? Four Mile Creek?"

"That's it," he said. "All hundred and sixty acres."

My father had not looked up, but he kept on eating. My mother looked at my father, then my brother, then back down at her plate. My nephew had left the table a few minutes back to get a glass of milk, and he had not returned.

"Why?" I asked.

"I'm going to let it go wild. Back to seed. I'll be able to come back, and bring friends back, and hunt. New Jersey hunting, it's not that much fun."

"I'd say," I said. I had piled up a dozen little black shot on the side of my plate from the single quail I had eaten. The shot were black and round, and I had stacked them like cannon balls on the lip of the plate. "I mean, what did you all do, hold the birds down and all of you shoot them? I've found twelve,...." I found another and brought it to my lips. "Thirteen shot I've found."

"Your brother says they don't even let you keep the ones you shot," Dad said. "You bring them in at the end of the day, isn't that right? and exchange them for ones they've dressed and frozen."

I looked at my brother and smiled. "That's not much different than going to the grocery store."

"That's why I am buying the farm," he said. "I can hunt my own birds, and clean them, and fish. I'll stock the pond...."

"When my grandfather owned the place, then the hunting was good, all around," my father said. The peas rolled off his fork.

"It will be good to come back to Ice's Crossing and hunt," my brother said.

"Better for you," I said. "Not so good for the birds." But I didn't begrudge him his hobby. But if he owned the farm, it could not be mine, it was no longer ours. He was buying up our past. "You bought the old place?" I asked again. "The farm at Four Mile?"

I looked at my father across the table, at my mother beside him. She was mashing quail meat on his plate as if to squeeze the black shot out of it. He still struggled with the peas, oblivious to my question, to the news. Maybe he already knew. Maybe he did not hear. Maybe it was fitting to him, perfectly right.

"It will be a way to get back to things," my brother said. "Back to the way things were. Like hunting," he said. "It will be real hunting."

He had that warm, broad, confident smile on his face behind which he was so terribly unknowable.

I only went hunting with my father once, in the fall before he sold the old place on Four Mile and moved us to town. My brother was off on a Boy Scout weekend, and it was fall, hunting season, not long after the World Series had been won and lost, and an end had come to summer farm work. It was that time in the year before my father took to the radio, as he did every winter, sitting by the stove in the living room as it glowed red, bent over and listening, twisting the dial and searching for a signal from somewhere distant. I could not make out the voices below the static. 'Cincinnati,' my father would say. 'I got a guy in Cincinnati.' Or, 'Del Rio. By god, that's Del Rio, Texas. Old Brinkley's station. And it's raining in Del Rio.' He would say it like he wished he was there, in Del Rio, outside, in the night, in the rain.

"It's a day for hunting," my father said. "Want to go?"

It was evening, and if we were going to hunt we had to get up at four and walk west along the ridge half a mile, then turn right and down the ridge to a place where the Four Mile Creek ran shallow and wide and there were reeds and moss along the banks, and sumac bushes and blackberries were thick in and among the old walnut trees. That was the grove in which my father liked to hunt, on the very edge of his land at the last wild spot.

"Me?" I said, surprised. I looked around for my brother, expecting him to be there, and that my father was asking him to go. "Brother's not here," I said.

"Just you," he said. "If you want to go along. Can't have no gun. You're too young. But you can come along."

Of course I would go. That evening we laid out the stuff to take, his gun, the ammunition, our jackets, boots, a special red hat I was to wear so I could be seen or more easily found, if need be. To give me something important to do, I was to carry the ammunition.

"Bullets won't blow up in his pocket, mother," my father said when she gave him that worried look.

I was up and dressed and ready all on my own an hour before he got out of bed. I had stoked the fire in the parlor to a warm heat and had a cup of coffee left over from the day before for him and one for me. I even made new coffee for the trip which I had put in an old thermos bottle. Then I sat and waited in the flickering of the wood stove, watching the fire through its thick glass. I was pleased he was pleased when he saw me dressed and ready and eager.

He said nothing, not then, nor while he drank his coffee, nor as he got his gun and left the house, me just a step or so behind. The frost on the grass was lit by the moon, and the stiff grass crackled as we walked. It was rare to have seen the day begin, and I was surprised to feel the world fall into its deepest quiet, into its heaviest slumber just as the light began to spread across the sky. The sharp clear skeletons of trees were beautiful, so stark against the clean new sky.

When we approached my father's favorite hunting spot, I could sense the pheasants nearby in their shrubs. Along the face of a hill too rocky to farm, too steep to graze, he stopped and squatted down on his haunches. His breath was quiet, but I could see the vapors in the morning chill. I could see him move his eyes about as if he could listen with them, as if he could hear the faint and rapid heartbeats of birds we knew were around us.

He broke his shotgun at the breach. "The shells," he whispered. "Two shells." He held up two fingers.

I knew then what sudden death was like. I knew for all the things that I had done, for all my careful preparations and waiting that morning, my dreams the night before, the dreams of this all my life, of hunting with my father, I knew what it must be to die suddenly and by surprise. I had failed. The shells were in their box, and the box was on the table in the kitchen a long, cold mile back home.

I looked at him. For a brief moment he did not know what I knew.

"I need two shells," he said, and he said it with a kindness and understanding, a kind of kinship and camaraderie he still felt, as if he was about to show me now some secret of manhood that would shape my life, while I knew then a door would shut that I could never open up again.

I did not look at him for more than a moment. Then I looked away, past him, at the path, and at the shrubs in the path, at the breakers where the pheasants were hiding. I couldn't look at him. I seemed to have the power now to look into the grass, into the tangle of blackberry bushes and I, too, could see the birds frightened, waiting, quieted. I, too, could hear them with ears that were buried in my heart. I stood, and as I stood and turned away I heard the fluttering inside the bushes, fluttering of a pheasant I had seen with all my newfound powers, fluttering and then it broke from cover, not flying high, for pheasants cannot truly fly, but it fluttered and flustered and coasted down the pathway away from us and into the dark and into other grass, and then it was gone.

I was walking home. I felt for the first time in my life pulled along, pulled back, as if water was rushing across my feet, as if I stood in the ocean and could feel the undertow, pulled to one side, but I walked on.

"You forgot the shells." Then louder. "You forgot the goddamned shells." And that in a tone that was to be the tone between us forevermore.

Ron Pullins lives and works on the North Shore of Massachusetts where he runs a small independent publishing company specializing in esoterica in Latin, Greek, Russian, philosophy and political science. Previous work has appeared in journals, including *Shenandoah, New Laurel Review,* and *Kansas Quarterly.* The excerpts here are from a recently finished novella, *Tiles.*

Denise Brennan Watson

FALSE CHARMS & CHITLINS

Get a cluster of sisters huddled over stainless sinks, and pop in an eight-track of Al Green singing "Love and Happiness," and people you see only at Christmas, Easter, and Juneteenth come out of the woodwork to get a whiff of Patty Jean's chitlins. Whenever we had chitlins at our house, folks my mother wasn't even on speaking terms with just happened to drop by to see how everybody was doing.

We didn't have 'em often because hours of patient picking, rinsing, and washing went into cleaning them, and they ended up being expensive because once we were through picking off all the sticks and ticks, slime and fat, there wasn't much "chitlin" left in the bucket. One fall day in 1973, my sisters and I had knelt over the sinks in green upholstered chairs until our knees stuck to the vinyl. The air hovering above the Gulf of Mexico lay like a blanket over our house, making October feel like the middle of July. Since we were stationed in the kitchen most of the day, we turned on the window unit to zap out some of the misery of that Texas heat.

At ages nine, ten, and twelve, my sisters and I were being initiated into a new rite of passage. We had filled two red plastic pails with watery gunk we picked off the intestines and had ten pounds yet to clean. Gretta was the oldest, and Mary and I let her clean the dirtiest ones. "OOO!" she screamed. "Look what I found. A dead bee and some kind of legs. Look like spider legs wrapped around it. Aunt Stella, do pigs eat bees?"

"Baby, pigs eat anything," she replied. "Ain't no tellin' what you'll find in a pig's stomach. Me and your Mama have seen much worse than that."

Gretta frowned as she picked at the insect cluster with her dainty, scalloped fingernails. Mary and I were jealous of Gretta's perfect nails. She paid no attention to them, didn't file them or paint them, yet they grew long and sculpted, just like Mama's and just like Aunt Stella's.

Aunt Stella took two packages of hog maws from the refrigerator and set them into a pan of cool water. When we had chitlins, we had to have plenty of hog maws. Mama would cut them into bite-sized pieces and cook them right along with the chitlins. They absorbed the taste of that good broth and made the meal go a lot further. Hog maws were cheaper and didn't require all that picking and scrubbing.

"Jean, remember when hog maws used t'..."

"Not now, Stella," Mama cut in. "Here's my song." Mama's eyes closed, and her head rocked from side to side like she was some place where she could not be reached. Rim shots tip-tapped a rhythm that made you wanna be Black if you weren't already, then Al broke in with "I'm Glad You're Mine." The organ haze mesmerized the air. Vocal chords dipped down low, then cut through with a falsetto that tempered Mama's pace down to a slow groove.

A grin that comes from a full, satisfied belly swept across her face. The beat snuck up from the center of the heat and took hold of her right foot. With hips swiveling and arms rocking, Mama joined in: *"Baay-beh... I'm sho glad y' heah. Baay-beh, I've got shumptin' t' shay, my deah."* Fingers snapped every beat and a half, turning Aunt Stella's patient grin into a full-blown laugh. Auntie forgot all about what she was gonna say about those hog maws. She shook her head and sealed the red buckets of gunk with white lids and packing tape.

"Pork Chit-ter-lings," I said, looking at the red letters on the flimsy white lids. "'Chit-ter-lings.' That doesn't even sound like food." The lids said "pre-cleaned." However, that never meant anything to any Black folks I knew. "Pre-cleaned" chitlins were just as filthy as the ones straight from the slaughterhouse. My job was rinsing and re-rinsing the chitlins Mary and Gretta had picked clean and washed.

"When does Cita get t' start cleaning off some of these insects, Mama?" Gretta asked as Mama returned to our world.

"She's too much like Howard Hughes t' be touchin' anything like that," she replied.

I didn't even like touching the "clean" chitlins. We didn't have antibacterial soap in those days, but I scrubbed my hands enough for everybody in the house put together.

Daddy never learned how to clean pork innards, but he sure knew how to make 'em disappear. He didn't even like to be around when we were cleaning them because the stench mated with the humidity, turning the kitchen air into something that smelled like a gutter.

"Where's Raymond?" my mother called from the kitchen to Uncle Skinny.

"You know he don't like t' be in here when y'all cleaning chitlins," he replied from underneath a white mustache laid on top of skin darkened over the years at Mr. Johnny's oil rig.

"Tell 'im t' fire up that pit 'cause I want 'im t' throw a few of these chitlins on the grill," she said. "We ain't had barbecued chitlins in I 'on't know how long. I know it was 'fo' the kids were born."

The door leading from the kitchen to the garage screeched open, and the sound of the dryer spinning Daddy's golf towels got louder. Standing in the doorway in denim overalls, Uncle Skinny had a smirk on his face. The matching ragged windows in his favorite outfit allowed his midnight-blue knees to show through. He wouldn't let Aunt Stella put patches on 'em. She used to chase him with a tomato pin cushion and a spool of thread, but she finally gave up and let him have his way.

Uncle Skinny always walked like he'd just gotten off a horse. Walking out the door, he raised his Falstaff can toward his thick, pink lips. His smirk became a grin, and teeth the color of dandelions parted. "Say, Ray-ee," he called. The door swung behind him, and the hum of the dryer faded into the background again.

"It's too hot t' be running the dryer, Patty Jean," said Aunt Stella, wiping liquid pearls from her forehead.

"He won't listen, Stella," said Mama. "All he care about is them golf clubs and them tournaments every time you turn around."

Knowing that Aunt Stella wasn't going to wash her hands after touching her forehead, I just pretended not to care. I knew better than to tell grown people to wash their hands.

Though it was officially fall, the air conditioning unit was still kicking full blast in Galveston, Texas. My parents grew up there, as did many of their relatives. Though my mother's baby brother, Gator, lived in town, Mama and Daddy rarely saw him unless they had something to offer him. Along with Gator's basketball fame with the NBA throughout the seventies and eighties came a sudden indifference to the roots which had given him his life and claim to blackness.

But he found a way to our house that day. He wasn't the type to knock on people's doors. He just walked on in like he lived there and helped himself to many of my parents' Flack and Hathaway, Aretha and Al Green tapes until the collection dwindled down to nearly nothing, like the chitlins. Uncle Skinny had seen him at the car wash the day before and mentioned that he and Aunt Stella were coming over for soul food. Uncle Skinny never did like Gator and wanted to rub his nose in some imaginary chitlins he could be eating if he hadn't left Mama and us kids in the rain at the grocery store two weeks before.

The aluminum screen door screeched open and creaked in stages until it finally shut. "Y'all cookin' chitlins?" Gator ducked down as he passed from the living room to the dining room, then looked around like he'd never been in our house before. He eyed the mound of raw intestines waiting for the kettle and an even larger mound yet to be cleaned. "I tell ya," Gator said, clamping his long narrow fingers on his right hip. "Y'all ain't even close."

With an ego bigger than Dallas, he carried shiny round tins of basketball footage shot during his beginning days underneath his left arm. We kids were usually the first to plop our behinds on the floor when Gator brought over his movies, but along with Mama, we were mad at him for leaving us in the rain at Kroger. Besides, we had work to do.

"Since ain't nothin' going on in this kitchen, guess I'll set up the machine, and we can watch the boy show that ball who is the real Papa," he said. He set his films down on the dining room table.

Mama took a deep breath and rolled her eyes toward the ceiling. Still making some mighty hefty breathing sounds, she looked at her watch. Mama turned her back to Gator and picked up the biggest knife in the kitchen. She laid it across her wooden cutting board whose surface was cracked and roughened from overuse. Two large onions sat on either side of the knife, and Mama pried her two-inch long fingernails under brown, papery skin until the onions were naked with skinny green stripes teasing down slick white flesh. Within seconds, two round onions had become two hundred precision-cut rectangles. She tucked a small pile of onions into a waxed sandwich bag and tossed the rest into the kettle on the blue flame. Mama's kettle was reserved for special occasions. It was her mother's and had become black over time from years of cooking for people joined by blood.

Mama's mother was Margaretta, but we all called her Mama Gretta. Boy, could she cook. Everything my mother knew about cooking, she learned from Mama Gretta. She'd been gone over two years, but it seemed like she'd never left. Her kettle was sitting on our stove, and Mama stood over it just as her mother had. Mama's shoulders sloped in the same way, and her slender, perfect hands flickered with the same spark.

Mama Gretta prepared many meals in our home, and even before I was born the kettle was part of our house. That was her "cookin' kettle," as she had called it. She and that kettle often filled our house with the smell of ham hocks and pinto beans, cabbage and bacon stew, turnips and minted onion, and spare ribs with braised potatoes. I learned at an early age how people and their pots and pans can bond together, as though they were born of the same flesh and bone.

There wasn't any friction between Mama and Aunt Stella over the kettle because Mama was the one who really loved to cook. Her sister didn't mind cooking, but Mama lived for frying, stewing, and greasing up some pans. Now the "cookin' kettle" lives at my house. I have invoked the spirit of Mama Gretta many times with golden drumsticks and batter-fried catfish cooked in her kettle. I have made chili, soups, stews and goulash in that all-purpose family gem.

Looking at that kettle on the blue flame that day, I wondered how Gator could show such disrespect in the presence of Mama Gretta. She was there as much as any of the rest of us, and was present in a more sacred way than any of us. Yet Gator showed no regard for his Mama, my Mama or that cookin' kettle which had fed him from birth on.

Gator still hadn't made eye contact with Mama, nor had he acknowledged the fact that she was there. "I have t' go out t' my Cad-Lac and get my projector," he said. "I cain't believe you Black folks don't have no projector." The back of Gator's head ducked down as he disappeared.

The screen door repeated its squealing and creaking sequence. Mama's mouth tightened, and she dug her fingernails into some of those chitlins. "Mary, lemme have summa yo' pile," she said. Gretta, Mary, and I retreated a little to give her some room. Mama's fingers moved fast, and her eyes narrowed to an intensity that made me uncomfortable.

We had been moving in the kitchen in a kind of round, unhurried way. Al Green, the dryer, the red pails, icy knuckles, Mama Gretta's kettle, the blend of Black voices moved in circles so that everything present was part of everything else. There was no reason to hurry or fuss. No reason to tighten up or change the pleasure of cooking with family into a series of quick motions and silent retreat.

Yet even Aunt Stella was alert in a way she hadn't been before. Her china-bone stature and slight shoulders were ready for something to break. She bit her lower lip and dug her hands into Gretta's pile of chitlins. Gretta, Mary, and I continued to work, wondering what was to come.

The bass came out of the background and thumped through the kitchen. I hadn't remembered Al's voice being that loud before. I felt sorry for him because he was just singing along, not aware that things had changed and that Mama's hips would not be swiveling.

The door creaked open, and before it could squeak shut, Gator banged against it, rattling the aluminum. A string of choice words flew out of his mouth. "Why don't y'all get a house? I have t' bend down every time I come in here."

Uncle Skinny came around from the backyard to see what all the commotion was. "Man, what choo doing here?" he demanded. "Didn't nobody tell you t' bring yo' black ass out here. You too good to come around, so why you here now?"

"Maybe I should go out there befo' they get into it," said Aunt Stella, breaking our silent spell. She scrubbed her hands with a bar of Jergens and dried them on her apron. The three of us girls took turns washing our hands and followed her with wet, wrinkled fingers, stopping at the screen door. We watched Aunt Stella, who was built like a child, trying to stand between two grown men.

"This ain't yo' house, man," said Gator, using his special high-pitched voice reserved for confrontations. "You ain't even blood."

"Yeah, well, yo' ass gone be blood if...'

"Y'all cut it out," pleaded Aunt Stella. Her glance cut over to the Cadillac then snapped back over to Gator.

Gator's lime-green car was parked on the curb. He had purchased it in cash as a Father's Day present to himself that year even though he didn't become a father until years later. The passenger door opened, and a pair of long, spindly tan legs came out. A woman with an Afro as big as Daddy's pepper bush got out of the front seat.

"That must be Marla," Mary whispered to us. Marla's raggedy jean shorts looked like they had been blown up with an air pump. With platformed feet and laced ankles, she teetered toward the driveway. A pair of sunglasses sat above burgundy lips.

"Honey, ain't nothin' here got nothin' t' do wit you," said Aunt Stella. "You can get on back in that car."

"You not gone talk t' my girl like that," Gator said, pitching his voice as high as he could. He turned to Marla. "Baby, wait in the car. I got t' set some things straight." When he talked to Marla, he sounded like a man. Marla spun around and headed back for the Cadillac.

"Stella, Honey," said Uncle Skinny. "I want you to go back in the house."

"Skinny, I ain't goin' back inside wit y'all carryin' on."

"Get this senior citizen out of my way befo' I act a fool," Gator said, waving off Uncle Skinny.

"Why do you have t' act out, Gator?"

"You not gone pull that on me, Stella. I didn't tell him t' come up in my face braggin' about a damn thing. Naw, but he got t' let me know everybody was gone be eatin' chitlins. Fine, if nobody wanna be bothered wit me, then t' hell wit y'all."

"Girls, git back in here t' this kitchen," called my mother. She didn't say "this instant," so we lingered at the door, waiting for that second call.

Aunt Stella's neck jerked back over toward the curb. She shot

79

Gator a look that was as direct as an ice pick. "Gator, it ain't like that. That's the way yo' childish mind see it. What makes you think you can just walk right in this house after the way you treated yo' own flesh and blood?"

Gator blew out some air and put both hands on his hips. He turned a tired glance toward Miss Cool sitting in the Cadillac. "It ain't my fault that fat sister of yours don't know how to drive a car."

"Gretta, Mary and Cita, I said 'git back in here t' this kitchen!'"

Leaning toward the kitchen, we chimed in unison, "We're coming." We held out for that last earful before we left the screen door.

"You promised Raymond 'fo' he left for that tournament you'd drive Patty Jean where she needed t' go. You just sorry, Gator. Cain't believe nothin' you say."

"I had bizness t' take care of. Besides, she had money for a taxi anyway, didn't she?"

"That don't have nothin' t' do wit it. You said you'd be there. You don't even care about these kids. All you care about is what benefits you. You cain't sacrifice nothin' for nobody."

"I ain't lisnin' t' yo' mess, Stella. You ain't my Mama."

"Why cain't you see that yo' family care 'bout you? We just want you t' act like you care, too."

Just as we turned from the door, Mama was walking our way. Her pace was quick. "When I tell you t' do something, I mean do it now. I don't wanna hear 'I'm coming, I'm on my way.' If y'all want me t' give ya somethin' t' cry about today, I can arrange that." Without a word, Mary, Gretta, and I returned to the kitchen and resumed our stations.

The tempo in the kitchen had changed. Lamenting chords seeped through the hi-fi webbing. Familiar voices crooned, *"Oh-hhh Girl, I'd be in trouble if you left me now, 'cause I don't know where t' look for love. I just don't know how."* When Mama got quiet and started listening to the Chi-Lites, we made sure we were doing what we were supposed to do.

Over and behind Mama's voice we'd heard Daddy and Uncle Skinny sharing some sharp words about their brother-in-law. Mama's jaws were tight and silent. She picked away at those chitlins, seemingly not seeing or hearing anything besides what she had in her hands and what she had brewing in her head. Even Daddy was in another frame of mind. He was so wrapped up in what he and Uncle Skinny were saying, he had forgotten that he couldn't stand the smell of dirty chitlins.

Pressure had been building up in my bladder, but I put it out of my mind by concentrating on the sounds of Daddy's and Uncle Skinny's voices.

"I mean it, Ray. I'm gone go upside that boy's head if he keep it up."

"Don't let that no-good chump get t' you. I didn't go out there 'cause I don't wanna have t' jack that Negro up. I'm not gone let that boy bring me down like that."

"You didn't know 'im when he was growing up, Ray. I bin puttin' up with that punk ever since Stella and me first started, and I be damn if I'm gone let him try t' make everybody else feel like some used poke chop. Leas' I know what work is. Leas' I remember who my family is."

I ran my hands across the Jergens and air-dried them as I left the kitchen. I must have been a sight to see, tiptoeing with my legs crossed all the way to the bathroom. I didn't get to hear the rest of what Aunt Stella and Gator were saying, and I didn't want anybody to say or do anything else until I got back. However, by the time I returned to the kitchen, Daddy and Uncle Skinny had returned to the backyard with the barbecue pit.

A car engine started up, and tires whistled down the street. Aunt Stella walked into the kitchen and wiped sweat from her face. Looking down at her apron, she held her hands across her brows. She collected herself as though she needed to before trusting herself to say anything. Water splashed in the sinks, and climate-controlled air hummed in from the window unit. Mary, Gretta, and I squirmed around, waiting for someone to say something, but half-hoping nobody would.

Mama continued to let out puffs of air as she concentrated on rocking that blade up and down and across a handful of jalapeños she had picked off Daddy's bush out back. Slender green peppers lost their stems and became a pile of dark green skin, seeds, and light green membrane. With her lips poked out in silence, Mama scraped the peppers into the kettle, scratching the blade across moist wood. She slid her thumb and index finger down the blade and flicked the seeds which had stuck to the knife into boiling water.

Harmonica chords blended with soft voices as the Chi-Lites painted pictures of Black men facing dilemma: pain, love, Black women, scraping by, providing for the family, running with the crowd, coming back home to love that'll be there no matter what. *"All my friends call me a foo-ool. They say 'let the woh-mun take care of you-oo.'"* That line turned Mama's huffing into crying. Aunt Stella's arm was wrapped around Mama's shoulders before the next piano riff could do any more damage.

"Baby, don't give him the honor. He ain't worth you feelin' like this."

"Why does he hate me, Stella? I've always been there for him, but he's never there for me. He ain't family. Family don't treat ya like that. All we have between us is blood."

"You know I have my own differences with him. But he is family. Lord knows we cain't change that. But he's family only when he want somethin' from somebody. You always family. Bad or worse, you always family. Give or take, you there for him, Jean. That's what he counts on. He knows you gone step in and clean up his mess no matter how he treat you."

"Well, it ain't gone be like that no mo'. He's split his pants for the last time."

"Patty Jean, you always say that, and he don't ever learn his lesson 'cause you don't stick t' yo' guns wit him. You got t' show him that he ain't running nothin' and he ain't gone mess all over you."

"I know. I'm just sicka... Gretta, go tell ya father not t' worry 'bout that pit. I'm not inda mood no mo'."

Gretta raised her glance from the steel sink to meet Aunt Stella's firm gaze.

"Child, we not gone let Gator or no other part-time nothin' ruin this meal. We here today on this Sunday the Lord give us t' be wit people we care 'bout and who care 'bout us. You go out there and take ya Daddy summa them chitlins y'all cleaned, and tell 'im t' throw 'em on the grill."

Gretta's downward cheeks and lips crept into something that wasn't quite a smile. Aunt Stella wasn't trying to put Mama out of her place, but she just always knew what was wrong and how to make things right. Gretta scooped some pork intestines into a pan.

"I'm ready for a little taste of some barbecued chitlins, myself," said Aunt Stella. "What about you, Jean?" Gretta was out the door before Mama could answer.

The dryer wasn't humming anymore. From the window above the sinks, I saw Uncle Skinny and Daddy sitting in vinyl crisscrossed lawn chairs we got with our Texas Gold Stamps. Orange and yellow sashes danced skyward out of the galvanized barrel. Quick blue tongues licked the air, giving the moment beyond the kitchen window an almost unreal, wavy look like the scene I was looking at was a cross between a mirage and a painting.

The expressions on their faces told me that there wasn't nearly as much heat in that pit as there was in the words they were passing. Daddy's eyes narrowed, widened and rolled sideways, cutting to the corners. His thin mustache curved into shapes forming around words unaccompanied by sound. Words no sooner spoken than remembered. Words that made his eyebrows, lips, and tongue flicker like flames burning some decree into the wind giving voice to his mind. Words that pulled me toward the window, then in my mind, to the other side of the glass suspended between dishrags and cut grass.

Uncle Skinny did most of the listening as he dragged thick, chapped hands across his chin. A conflicting blend of disgust and family duty stung his eyes into confusion. His lids lowered, then peeled skyward. His mouth sort of hung open as if to say "Hell if I know." Silence fell on both of them, though to me it sounded just the same. After a spell, Uncle Skinny tapped Daddy on his khaki-clad knee, and his mouth closed into a smile. He clapped his hands in the air and leaned forward in his chair, showing his dandelion teeth. All of a sudden, it looked like they both had something to smile about.

Gretta crept into my view, stepping down the path Daddy made. She watched her feet move from stone to stone as she cradled the pan like a baby. Daddy and Uncle Skinny looked up as she approached them. Gretta handed the chitlins to Daddy, and he lowered the lid of the barrel to tame the flame down some.

Mama and her sister hugged. "I know you right, Stell. What matters is what we've been blessed wit today. We got some burnin' t' do. Mama Gretta wouldn't have it no other way." Aunt Stella reached for the stereo. "Let's get this show going and give our mood some food for the soul." Donny Hathaway's fingers rippled across some ivory, setting the tone for the rest of the day. Roberta Flack's voice was like a tall glass of iced lemonade rehydrating a parched throat.

Comforting doesn't quite capture what she and Donny did in our house, in our bodies, our spirit that day. Comforting, soothing, healing. Yeah, all of that. *"Our time's short and precious, your lips warm and luscious. You don't have to wear false charms, 'cause when I wrap you in my hungry arms, be real Black for me. Be real Black for me."*

Mama washed her hands and started cutting the hog maws into small pieces. "What were you gone say 'bout hog maws earlier, Stella?"

"I wasn't gone say nothin', Jean. Nothin' that is as important as what I'm feelin' now," she said with a smile so tender it could have broken into crying.

In my head, I kept hearing *"Your hair's soft and crinkly. Your body's strong and stately. You don't have to search in Rome, 'cause I got your love at home. Be real Black for me. Be real Black for me."* I liked the way their voices overlaid and completed each other and the way Mama responded to the music. Her humming came from somewhere down deep. The more she hummed, the more I understood why Aunt Stella had played that tape. Just as the song faded out, Mama hit the button and played it again.

Denise Brennan Watson was born in Corpus Christi, Texas and has lived in Minnesota and Ohio. She is the author of *The Undertow of Hunger*, a collection of food poems published by Finishing Line Press in 1999. She holds an M.A. in philosophy from Miami University and is a member of The Honor Society of Leap Year Babies, an international organization based in Keizer, Oregon.

"False Charms & Chitlins" is her first piece of fiction. She was inspired to write it after having read *Devil in a Blue Dress* by Walter Mosley.

YEAH, BUT CAN SHE COOK?

Stuart Rumpleman looked at his plate and wanted to cry. He should be savoring a two-inch thick sirloin steak, lightly charred on the outside but still pink in the middle. Or a slice of prime rib awash in its juices. Or a simple bacon, lettuce and tomato sandwich, smothered in mayonnaise, heavy on the bacon. He should be digging into a mound of fried clams, shrimp and scallops. Or devouring a turkey drumstick, leg of lamb, or southern fried chicken breast. At the very least, he should be squeezing a lemon slice over a nice pound of fish, that healthiest member of the meat food group.

What he wouldn't give right now for a piece of haddock, flounder or swordfish. Or if he could really have his pick of the aquatic litter, he'd go for the sautéed Florida pompano that he'd devoured at a place called the Reef Grill while vacationing in West Palm Beach. Or dolphin, which he'd called mahi-mahi ever since a blind date confused it with a porpoise and got nasty.

"You're going to eat Flipper?" she had asked incredulously, looking suddenly ill. Several minutes of labored explanations had ensued about how Flipper was a porpoise, a mammal. And how he'd never eat a porpoise. As opposed to dolphin, which was just a fish, albeit amazingly succulent. Stuart's date that evening had seemed to grudgingly accept his explanation until their meals had arrived and he'd offered her a bite to prove his point. She'd excused herself for the ladies' room, never to return.

Which actually hadn't been a loss at all. She'd been quite a bore up to that point and her filet mignon, not to mention the baked potato stuffed with sour cream, had been exquisite. As blind dates went, Stuart Rumpleman gave it two thumbs up.

But now as he gazed forlornly at his plate, he thought briefly about how this time he'd even sink his teeth into good old Flipper. Ranger Porter Ricks, Bud and Sandy would have to make do in beautiful Coral Key Park without their aquatic star. Stuart Rumpleman's carnivorous taste buds needed Flipper more than the fans of the old TV show. Or at least it seemed that way, because what confronted him now was a bowl of artichoke soup and a plate full of grilled tofu, lima beans and rutabagas.

Stuart forced as broad a smile as he could muster, nodded, and said, "Looks great."

Tia beamed.

He was a carnivore, for crying out loud. Those sharp incisors were made for tearing meat, not tofu. His salivary glands didn't react to a rutabaga. They reacted to a Big Mac, a Whopper, or a Wendy's bacon double cheeseburger. Or even better, one of each. This vegetarian swill just wasn't natural. After his first day with Tia, all that roughage had given him so much gas that a single match lit anywhere near him could have blown up most of Boston. Admittedly, his digestive system had eventually adjusted. He was over the natural gas crisis. But he wasn't over the craving.

Why couldn't he deny himself and still be happy? This was, after all, the Woman of His Dreams. And meat repulsed her. He could handle one vegetarian meal, no problem. Or two or three. But they'd been together for over a month now. Thirty-three days, not that he'd been counting.

He hadn't touched meat for thirty-three days. Not for breakfast, lunch or dinner. Not for snacks. Not when he was with Tia. Not when he was away from her. Thirty-three days! And he was no mere fan of food. As his doctor had once said in exasperation, Stuart didn't eat to live. He lived to eat.

And in the last month, food had become an endless stream of eggplant and radicchio sandwiches, cabbage cakes, lentil soup, turnips, tofu, braised onion and mushroom stir-fry, gingered leek and fennel flans, Brussels sprouts and broccoli pesto.

What was on tap for tomorrow? Eggplant upside-down spinach with a split-pea crust? It was all his fault, of course. He stabbed a lima bean with his fork and began to chew.

"Would you mind terribly if I joined you?" she asked.

Stuart had been sitting alone at a table at T. Anthony's, a popular pizzeria on Boston's Commonwealth Avenue. A Boston University hockey game had just let out and the place was packed. He had just placed his order—a large pizza with pepperoni, sausage and ham—when she walked in.

She was the most astonishing creature he'd ever seen. With a model's face, high cheekbones and perfect white teeth, a to-die-for body that a single glance confirmed was perfect in every way, and long, flowing blonde hair.

Stuart, who looked like a middle-aged version of Flounder, the misfit in the movie ANIMAL HOUSE, felt his heart slip into arrhythmia. This goddess was talking to him. Was asking to join him. A cardiac infarction seemed imminent. His mouth became dry, his tongue like a wad of cotton. This didn't happen to guys like him. Nothing happened to guys like him.

"Actually, I was reserving this seat for someone really attractive," he heard himself saying to his utter disbelief. "But I guess you'll do."

She blinked. There was silence for what seemed like minutes. And then she burst out laughing.

"Humor really is the ultimate aphrodisiac, don't you think?" she asked, sitting down. "By the way, my name is Tia."

Hearing the word aphrodisiac pass her lips made him dizzy.

"Humor is like the nectar of the gods," he said, in an exaggerated Harvardian fashion, to his further self-amazement. Then he grinned.

Where had that come from? He'd never been able to carry on small talk before, but here he was with the most divine creature who'd ever deigned to speak with him and, while it wasn't exactly material that would get him invited on Letterman, his chatter was somehow amusing her. Her blue eyes sparkled. Her white teeth flashed as her laughter echoed in his ears. She was physical perfection.

And in no time, Stuart Rumpleman knew that Tia was not just exquisitely beautiful, she was his soul mate. She loved John D. MacDonald's Travis McGee novels and all but the earliest William Goldman. She not only read short stories—that alone made her one in a million—but she too, considered Harlan Ellison the art form's most accomplished practitioner since Poe.

She loved Casablanca and all the other old Humphrey Bogart films, even though they were in (gasp!) black and white. And her "Here's looking at you, kid," impersonation was almost as bad as Stuart's.

She could then gracefully slide into the time-honored debates of Ted Williams vs. Joe DiMaggio, Bill Russell vs. Wilt Chamberlain, Jim Brown vs. Gail Sayers and she knew that Bobby Orr vs. anybody was a waste of time and breath. She adored Bach's Brandenburg Concerto No. 2, and Charlie Parker's "Ornithology" while still remaining a fan of Aerosmith and the Black Crowes.

Stuart wondered fleetingly what this astonishing creature could possibly see in a nebbish like himself. Then he banished the thought. He would not be like Groucho Marx, refusing to join any club that would have him as a member. Perhaps opposites attracted, after all. Beauty and the Beast, right? And after all, some women found Jack Nicholson attractive, didn't they?

He and Tia were tuned to the same wavelength. In the space of minutes, they had forged a link that dreams were made of. They were really, truly, honest-to-goodness, right for each other. Suddenly, she put her hand on his and a pained look came to her face.

"Please, please, tell me that you don't eat meat," she said. "I could never love someone who eats animals. Meat is just so repulsive. Dairy products, I could accept. I don't touch them myself, but I try to have an open mind. But meat..." She shuddered in disgust.

He blinked, and licked his lips. His tongue felt like cotton.

"It's immoral, too, when you consider its effect on world hunger," she continued. "It's ethically bankrupt, that's what it is. You are a vegetarian, aren't you?"

Stuart Rumpleman suddenly experienced a foxhole conversion. Like soldiers who made good with their maker as they stared death in the face, Stuart looked into Tia's blue eyes and swore to himself that he would never touch meat again. Broccoli and spinach and cucumbers were his friends.

"Of course," he heard himself say. "The health benefits alone are indisputable. It's astonishing that anyone eats flesh these days. It's... it's practically barbarian!"

He wondered for a moment if this new small talk voice inside his head was laying it on too thick, but the concern proved baseless.

"I'm so relieved!" she said and ran a finger along his palm. Suddenly, the foxhole convert felt a chill go up and down his spine. The pizza! He couldn't very well bring his pepperoni, sausage and ham pizza back to the table after having just espoused the virtues of a vegetarian lifestyle. They had to get out of here and fast.

"You want to go somewhere else?" he asked.

"Sure. How about my place?" she asked. "It's just two blocks from here and I'm a great cook."

After the first totally vegetarian meal of Stuart's life, he and Tia continued their feast in the bedroom. Food had always held a near-erotic quality for him, but it had never actually been part of a sexual experience.

But on this night, Tia showed him things he'd never even imagined, and he had imagined a lot. And when he thought it couldn't get any better, she directed the piece de resistance. At her behest, he placed pineapple rings on her breasts so that her nipples poked out of the circular holes. Stuart then poured lightly warmed Hershey's chocolate syrup into the empty center of the each pineapple slice, covering Tia's nipples.

He then licked the syrup off as she shuddered, and nibbled the pineapple. When she returned the favor in the strategically optimal place, Stuart knew that his cheeseburger days were over.

Except that they weren't. He was in love with this goddess, no question about it. The sex wasn't just great. It was mind-boggling. It wasn't all pineapples and chocolate syrup. Sometimes it was just good old-fashioned coitus. But that was unbelievable, too.

They were eating like rabbits and mating like rabbits. And it wasn't just sex, as if there'd be anything wrong with that. They were making love, experiences that were both intensely physical and at the same time powerfully emotional, bordering on the spiritual. He'd always considered that sort of thing to be the stuff of bad romance novels and sappy chick flicks. But it didn't feel that way to Stuart now. For an ugly duckling who had never been loved, his transformation into a swan, at least in Tia's eyes, filled a lonely emptiness that he'd felt in his heart for as long as he could remember. He was happier than he ever could have imagined. Except...

Except he couldn't get his mind off what Tia considered the forbidden fruit. Every cell in his body cried out for meat. A filet mignon. A drumstick. Anything but this Brussels sprouts and turnips crap that Tia insisted on seven days a week.

It had nothing to do with that oldest of sexist phrases that guys used after hearing about the perfect woman: "Yeah, but can she cook?" He'd gladly cook, just like he had all his adult life. He could marinate some steak tips or fry some sausage. He could grill anything from shrimp to swordfish. Unfortunately, however, he knew nothing about cooking with celery, cucumbers or bean curd. Could you fry a turnip? Could you grill a rutabaga? To cook a meal in this bewildering meatless world would expose that he was a fraud.

Besides, Tia was a spectacular cook, if you liked that sort of thing. And to be honest, he could probably adjust to squash and zucchini and all their boring relatives if only there wasn't at the same time a fence around the entire animal kingdom. Adam and Eve had their forbidden Tree of the Knowledge of Good and Evil that they couldn't stay away from. Pandora had her box that she just had to open. And Stuart Rumpleman still lusted for meat.

Eventually he strayed. He was at lunch with some of his associates at work. They had just polished off a big presentation and were out celebrating on the corporate tab. He'd raised a few eyebrows in recent weeks with his sudden affection for the plant kingdom, but today they seemed more preoccupied with their own choices and blowing off the steam built up during work on the presentation.

The menu seemed to read meat, meat and then some more meat. As his co-workers began to order all the foods that his body craved, his salivary glands revved into warp overdrive. One time wouldn't hurt, he told himself.

"I could never love someone who eats animals."

She isn't here and what she doesn't know won't hurt her, he thought. She isn't my mother. "Please, please tell me that you don't eat meat." When we eat them, vegetables probably scream in pain, too. "Meat is just so repulsive."

It's really none of her business, he thought. The voice of Tia in his head became silent.

"I'll have the prime rib, king size, medium rare," he said. "And I'll also have the fisherman's platter."

"There goes the budget!" muttered Carl, his boss, chuckling.

"I'll pay for it myself!" snapped Stuart, to whoops of laughter around the table.

"Don't forget the Diet Coke," added Carl with a grin.

Stuart ignored his boss.

"And bring me the shrimp cocktail while we wait," he added. "I could eat a horse."

When the food arrived, he barely came up for air.

Tia slapped him hard across the face, knocking him back against the bedroom wall. He fell to the floor. He looked up in amazed silence. He had unlocked the door to her apartment and, at the sound of her voice, rushed to the bedroom. He had decided that he wouldn't announce his transgression. What she didn't know wouldn't hurt her. Perhaps this would even be the ideal solution: he would live like a vegetarian around Tia and maintain a secretly carnivorous side away from her.

As he entered the bedroom, he stopped and shook his head in amazement and delight. She was dressed in Victoria's Secret regalia from the best pages of the lingerie catalog: black lace that was cut low in the right places and cut high in the right places. She wore a sinfully wicked look on her face that told him there was yet another erotic surprise in store, another pleasure boundary to cross. He kissed her lips and pressed his body against hers.

And then she belted him.

In another circumstance, the look of pure fury on her face might have appeared incongruously funny, considering her attire. But there was nothing funny about her glare and the hurt in her eyes and the sinking feeling Stuart felt in the pit of his stomach.

"You didn't!" she hissed.

"What are you, nuts?" he asked, conjuring some righteous indignation as he climbed to his feet.

"Don't be obtuse!"

She knew. Somehow she knew. Deny it, he thought. She has no proof. Even if she can read it on your face or hear it in your voice, your only hope is to deny it.

"Obtuse about what?" he asked.

"Give me my key and get out."

"What have I done? What's wrong with you?"

"I want the key." She began to cry. "I thought you were happy."

"I've never been happier in my life!"

She stopped crying and glared. "Then I hope it was worth it."

"I haven't done anything!" he said, his voice sounding increasingly shrill.

"I can smell it," she said softly. A chill went up and down Stuart's back.

"I can smell a meat-eater a mile away," she said. "You chewed your breath mints, but your entire body reeks of beef. You disgust me. Give me the key, leave and don't come back. Ever. You're a pig and I apologize to swine everywhere for lumping them in with you. You're beneath reproach."

Stuart swallowed hard. How could he have thrown away…

"I want the key," she said firmly.

Suddenly, a lifetime of lima beans and turnips didn't look so confining, especially not with a dessert that included nibbling strategically-placed pineapple rings and slowly licking chocolate sauce off Tia's nipples.

"It was just one slip," he pleaded, realizing that he sounded pathetic but not knowing what else to say. "I'll never do it again."

"You'll do it again and you know it."

Stuart Rumpleman stared at her. She was right. He would do it again. It was in his bones. It was in his cells. It was in his brain. Even though she had offered him his one chance at the Holy Grail of True Love, love with someone who had no business slumming with him, he still knew that if given a second chance, he'd eventually throw it away again. He'd last a month next time. Maybe two. Maybe three. Maybe even a year, although that seemed incomprehensible. But he'd throw it away again.

Slowly, sadly, he fished the apartment key out of his pocket.

"Can't you forgive me? I..."

What could he say? Even if he didn't believe it, could he say that he just needed time to change? That he simply had to adjust to being a vegetarian? That he'd been a fraud from the first moment they'd met? That someday he might be able to become deserving of her, even though right now he represented everything that she found repugnant?

"Please?" he begged.

"I forgive your deceit," she said coolly. "But I could never be attracted to you again. Now you disgust me and that can never change. It's that simple. That's how I am. That's what I told you when we first met. "So please leave."

Stuart Rumpleman sat alone in a booth at an all-you-can-eat buffet. He'd been through the line six times already and showed no signs of slowing down. What was the old phrase, he wondered, that it is better to have loved and lost than never to have loved at all? What a crock! He knew in the deepest levels of his soul that he could never be happy again. Any relationship he ever had for the rest of his life would pale by comparison. Nothing else would ever match up. And other than Tia, women hadn't exactly been flocking to him over the years.

All he'd be left with was his guilt at having thrown away his one chance at the Holy Grail. He'd been modestly unhappy before he met Tia, but he'd become comfortable with his life over the years. He'd accepted that he was Flounder from Animal House, possessing neither the looks nor the personality to attract the love of anyone.

Tia had exposed that vulnerable underbelly and then ripped the stiletto of lost love through it. Better to have loved and lost? Not in a million years. And to think that it had all gone up in smoke because she'd smelled it. Even when trapped in the web of his own fraud, he hadn't crashed like some carnivorous Casanova in a blaze of gluttonous glories. He'd gone down like a Flounder. Exposed because he reeked of beef. Guilty by virtue of smelling bad, your honor. Which meant that if he left the buffet right now—which he probably should, pig that he was—and passed any orthodox vegetarians, they'd be cringing at his very smell. Didn't that just sum up his whole life in a nice, neat package?

Suddenly, Stuart dropped his fork and stopped chewing. What the...?

Something didn't fit. Something didn't make sense. Tia had caught him because she'd smelled the beef. That's what she'd said and he didn't doubt it for a second. But if that were true, then back when they first met she'd have been able to tell even more easily that he was no vegetarian. If one meal's indiscretion could be detected, then surely she had known his true nature from her first sniff. She'd known back then at T. Anthony's that not only was he not a vegetarian, but the direct opposite.

Had this all been a setup? Stuart felt sick to his stomach. Had she selected him for a unique brand of torture, like watching an alcoholic fight off the sweats every time he walks past a bar? Had Tia, the Dominatrix of Diet, gotten her jollies from having a ringside seat at his destruction? Had he been just the latest in a long line of helpless misfits?

Stuart Rumpleman shook his head and sighed. He reached for the steak sauce.

Dave Hendrickson has been writing for about 25 years. He is best known as a sports writer for uscollegehockey.com and as an associate of ESPN.com. He has also covered the Boston Bruins and has written for numerous sports magazines. He is wildly handsome and humble to a fault, traits that are seldom recognized by his wife Brenda, daughter Nicole, and son Ryan.

About "Yeah, But Can She Cook?", Mr. Hendrickson says, "Most of the time when I'm asked how a particular idea originated, I adopt a deer-in-the-headlights look and respond, 'It just popped into my head.' In this instance, however, the germ of the story is easy to identify. I'd recently gotten some unpleasant medical news that was forcing major changes in my diet. As a veteran gourmand, I was not pleased at having to abandon my swinish ways. This story was an inevitable outgrowth of my own frustrations."

MUSICAL INTERLUDE

Lip-puckering melodies shouted with flutes and strings
tear the hair from my head, raise my temperature,
activate my salivary glands.
I feast on Vivaldi, Telemann, and Stamitz.

The Chamber Orchestra of Spoleto
transports me backward in time and age
to childhood in Ohio and West Virginia.
End-of-summer goodbyes were punctuated
with full hampers of picnic refreshments.
I helped grind sharp cheddar cheese with nuts and raisins
for a spread that would withstand late-summer's heat.

A crescendo revives the tongue-tingling taste
of persimmons discovered in North Carolina.
November's frost sweetens this succulent fruit.
I race with skittering squirrels through autumn's leaves
searching for the soft spheres, sucking tart juices.

Now I recall my first bite of fresh-picked kumquat
carving a keen appetite in mellow tropical sun.

I claim a close connection between the icons
of musical communication and quince conserve.
Lemon and nuts blended with cinnamon and nutmeg
are the grace notes for the tart green fruit.

I envision clear glass jars of cucumber
drenched with dill plucked from tall fronds
of dill lace, taste again the cut odor of seeds
between my teeth. Pour boiling water over-all
to marinate, and taste each week to discover
when they are ripe for eating.

My musicians serve this disparate banquet
of memory filled with salivary messages.
They parade through aural passages to my brain
whenever flutes and strings join to celebrate.

Marylin Lytle Barr's poetry may be found in literary journals and in her poetry books *Drawn From the Shadows*, *Concrete Consider-ations*, and *Unexpected Light*. She writes from her heritage in New England, from her emotional roots in the Catskill Mountains, and from thirty years of residency in New York City. A member of the Alchemy Club in Grahamsville, NY, the International Women's Writ-ing Guild, and the Catskill Art Society, Marylin shares her poetry on a continuous basis through readings, workshops, conferences, and on a one-to-one basis. Her *Arts Gallery* in Grahamsville is open by appointment for exhibition of some 100 of her art works which in many cases show the poetry that inspired them.

YIELD

She makes them still, recipes serving eight
or ten or twelve. It's what she is, the stroganoff,
the lasagna. She herself now dislikes food,
the empty table, nibbles crust while rearranging
curdled quarts of milk, bronze cold cuts
oxidizing green, pork chops—her husband's
favorite. Sleepless, she bruises garlic and pulls
the beards from mussels. Morning at the gargling
disposal; she marries ketchup from two family-
sized bottles. A habit. A necessary lie.

If there was ever a way to cook for one,
she can't remember or who she was exactly
when she knew. Her babies, grown
and quarrel-scattered, come back only in dreams
to search the freezer, asking, "What is there to eat?"
She pleads, "I'll make you anything you want,"
then wakes, plugs in the twelve-cup coffee pot.
She writes a list of what's gone bad, what's gone,
then shops, avoiding contents that have settled
and check-out clerks who ask, "Will this be all?"

The years flip backwards, indecipherable
as journal pages from that honeymoon
to Greece—she's forgotten her shorthand.
What she remembers now are the requests,
the favorite birthday dinners of each child,
the man she fed for thirty years who loved her
mashed potatoes, who walked out one day.
She's kept his dinner warm for seven months,
her fingers thinning, wedding band so loose
it falls into the angelfood cake batter.

Beth Ann Fennelly is from Chicago, and was educated at the University of Notre Dame, the University of Arkansas, and the University of Wisconsin. Currently, she is an Assistant Professor of English at Knox College in Galesburg, Illinois. She has published poems in *TriQuarterly*, *The Kenyon Review*, and *Best American Poetry 1996*.

Ms. Fennelly wishes readers to know that "Why I Can't Cook for Your Self-Centered Architect Cousin" gives a good recipe for pesto. The measurements are: 2 c. basil, 3 cloves garlic, 1/4 c. pine nuts, 1/4 c. olive oil, 1/2 c. parmesan cheese, and (optional) 1/2 t. salt. "Yield" was previously published in *The American Scholar*.

MY MOTHER'S EATING LESSONS

"Don't talk when you eat!" my mother snapped whenever I tried to speak at the dinner table. That was her daily mantra.

It wasn't always that way. As an infant in my high chair, I babbled away while I ate everything my mother fed me. She had to force-feed my older sister, squashing her mouth open to shove in the food, but I would eat forever—*as long as she talked to me.* Children were a burden, she told us often enough, but what would the neighbors say if one of hers died of starvation!

"What did you talk about when you were feeding me?" I ventured years later when I visited her, retired and deflated in Florida.

"I don't know," she intoned in her Yiddish accent. "Maybe about the old country or things I had to do that day. Relatives or the weather. I don't remember. Why do you ask so many questions!" My mother's impatience hadn't changed in five decades.

I don't remember those halcyon days of highchair dialogue. I do remember the daily injunction. It was the only one of her all-consuming regulations I couldn't seem to learn.

Sepia photographs show me a chubby baby but a skinny child. I guess that's when I began feeding myself and all talking stopped. I remember one particular evening straining my ribs against the green Formica table, bursting to tell my parents and sister that I'd won the elementary school spelling bee. But I couldn't risk being humiliated in mid-sentence.

So I learned to be silent, sometimes, when the risk was too high, even though my head was exploding.

"Why weren't we allowed to talk at the dinner table?" I asked my mother on her last visit to California.

"To be sure you chewed your food well. Why are you always criticizing me? I did the best I could. You try working eight hours a day in a suffocating factory surrounded by hundreds of pounding sewing machines. Then shop and cook dinner. You'd want some peace and quiet too."

My mother acquired her survival mentality early as one of those "starving children in Europe"—in Poland during World War I—who rummaged through garbage grateful for orange rinds or stale bread. Or so she reminded us whenever we picked at our plate: "You should be grateful to have any food at all!" The three of us, even my father who grew up poor in Russia, were sufficiently shamed and dug in.

We had reason to dawdle over my mother's meals. Because of her "nervous stomach"—acquired from those garbage days—she never used herbs or spices and rarely any salt, so her cooking ranged from bland to tasteless. In my mother's book, nutritional sustenance was the only reason for eating—not just to keep her from being shamed by our dying but also to keep us from getting sick—so she wouldn't lose a day's pay or even—god forbid!—her job.

All my mother's dinners replicated the balanced diet taught by the Yiddish daily newspaper *The Forward*—always a green vegetable, a starch, and a protein. Invariably, the vegetable was spinach, string beans, or peas and carrots, which, because of our small icebox, my sister and I purchased fresh and prepared every day after school. Occasionally, the green was replaced by a salad of sliced iceberg lettuce drenched in vinegar. The starch was always potatoes, boiled or mashed, and the protein was usually mackerel. When we complained, she said it was "good for us" and cheap. As predictable and tedious as the food was, eventually I wiped my plate clean: I was always hungry—but also it was *required*.

We also had to eat everything *fairly*.

"Eat your vegetables, eat your potatoes," my mother ordered as she surveyed my plate to be sure I consumed my rations in equal proportions, no matter how disproportionate the original servings. I *was* a sickly child, with mysterious fevers and a heart murmur, so she was more vigilant with me than with my sturdier sister. Sometimes I yearned to stuff myself with the best of that tepid fare, something wonderful like foamy mashed potatoes dabbed with butter or sour cream, but it was impossible to "cheat." So early on I learned to conclude every meal with one mouthful of each food left on my plate. Compliance became automatic.

The daily mackerel regime was interrupted on Fridays when my mother served a kosher Sabbath chicken, the only remnant of her Orthodox *shtetl* upbringing. She didn't even light candles, whether out of bitterness for the god who denied her an education and a happy marriage or just plain poverty, I never knew. Every week around 4 o'clock, my sister and I tossed the cut-up bird into a pot of water, added an onion, a clove of garlic, a few carrots and potatoes, then let the whole concoction simmer on the stove until my mother got home from work. By the time we sat down to eat, the chicken and vegetables just about disintegrated on contact. The real treat on Fridays was a freshly baked challah, its soft eggy sweetness contrasting with the stern rye bread and pumpernickel we ate on weekdays.

"Don't drink when you eat" was another of my mother's commandments. A tempting glass of milk was my reward *after* the meal. How else would I have room for the nutritious food she was spending her hard-earned money on? Besides milk, the only other liquid we were allowed to drink was orange juice. Milk was good for our teeth, juice prevented colds. The milk was delivered to the front door in bottles, the rich cream bulging up the lids during the winter months. I poured it over cold cereal for breakfast, guzzled it after school with dry homemade cookies, and sipped it lukewarm at bedtime. The freshly squeezed orange juice that greeted my sister and me every morning was my father's handiwork, documenting his existence before he left for the factory.

Desserts were also Spartan affairs, alternating between canned fruit cocktail and my mother's lumpy apple sauce, which she colored and sweetened slightly with a teaspoon of strawberry Jell-O, a unique concession to taste and aesthetics. Sugar was forbidden—it was bad for our teeth—with rare but thrilling exceptions, like a popsicle breathlessly purchased with a precious nickel before the trilling ice cream truck disappeared down our short street. Like the five-cent box of Jujifruits my reluctant sister shared with me at Saturday matinees. Like chocolate pudding, such a luxury that we vied to lick the pot.

I always knew my parents' piecework paychecks were flush with overtime when I smelled treats like lamb chops sizzling in the broiler, crisp breaded veal cutlets frying in Crisco on the stove, or paprika-coated brisket gurgling in the oven. Or on weekends, for breakfast, her pasty oatmeal replaced by toasted bagels smothered in cream cheese with slivers of smoked salmon, or mounds of pancakes dribbled with "anjemima" syrup; or for lunch a fried egg eclipsed by corned beef sandwiches smeared with mustard and scrunched with Jewish pickles.

But the real treat of my childhood was eating out. Rarely did that mean going to a restaurant. When it did, we'd trolley downtown to a Horn & Hardart's cafeteria where I'd gleefully deposit nickels and dimes into slots next to the gleaming rotating shelves of food—always for hot dogs and baked beans—or to the Cathay Tea Garden hung in exotic black and red tassels—always for chicken chow mein. But the real excitement of eating out was going to a relative's for dinner. At least once a month that meant going to my aunt's house, a two-story wonder of rooms, with a front lawn with beach chairs and trees and a back yard blessed with a sand box, slide, and jungle gym.

My mother's younger sister was a cheerful if imperious person. Blessed with an entrepreneur husband, she didn't have to work and loved to cook for him and their two small sons. From her packed refrigerator—no icebox for her!—came edibles that made my knees tremble, my mouth water—medium-rare steaks and buttered corn on the cob, juicy hamburgers and salted French fries, succulent lamb heaped with wild rice, and sauce-smothered spaghetti rampant with seasoned meatballs. I gobbled unfamiliar vegetables like broccoli and Brussels sprouts, cauliflower and zucchini, and downed salads made with thick green leaves, taut tomatoes, and crunchy cucumbers, all coated with a tangy dressing. I stuffed my mouth with tart cheeses and guzzled sodas—*sodas!* And for dessert, there was always Neapolitan ice cream, which I scooped endlessly and swathed in chocolate syrup. Even the coffee table offered a variety of snacks—from Hershey's kisses to hard candies, from Oreos to chocolate chip cookies, from nuts to potato chips—*potato chips!* I thought my little cousins lived in an enchanted castle.

The highlight of all this splendor was the respite from my mother's regulations. No admonishments against talking, no reminders not to drink during the meal, no scrutiny of equal proportions. At my aunt's house I stuffed my mouth and talked with it full without fear of my mother's yelling at me. I even raided the refrigerator without worrying that leftovers were needed for the next day's meal or bag lunches. I didn't understand my mother's silence, but I sensed her fear of her wealthy and generous baby sister. What a joy it was to hear her scorn my mother's attempts to stifle us: "Shirley, leave them alone! Let them eat!"

Then, there was the pleasure of eating out at my great-aunt's house, my mother's aunt, twice a year, on Rosh Hashanah and Passover. On those holidays, my mother's huge Polish immigrant family squeezed down the length of several bridge tables in what had been, hours before, my great-aunt's discount shoe emporium, with its bargain tables shoved back against the walls, now a mini-banquet hall. Surrounded by all her gussied-up elders and peers who had fared better than she had in the New World—all ladies of leisure with successful husbands—my mother sat obedient, sometimes actually smiling.

At first I joined the mad rush of feasting on all the traditional foods piled high on steaming platters—gefilte fish or chopped chicken liver, thick vegetable soup or beet borscht with sour cream, potato kugels or *kreplach,* and herb-roasted chicken that didn't fall apart on touch. The aunts and uncles kibitzed, the cousins squealed, everyone gleefully stabbing for seconds and thirds.

But long before the food was gone, I'd slip off my chair, exhausted and unsettled by all the unfamiliar chatter. I had got used to my mother's no-talking rule, retreating into the safety of its silence. Furtively, I'd climb to the second-floor bedrooms and run my fingertips over chenille bedspreads, fragile perfume bottles, and silver-scrolled picture frames. Sometimes, breathlessly, I tiptoed up to the dusty third-floor attic, braving the dimly lit and silent room to marvel at the hundreds of shoe boxes shelved from floor to ceiling.

By the time I returned to my seat, the adults were ensconced in the kitchen, sipping hot tea from tall glasses and nibbling sugar cubes, or jammed into the tiny living room playing poker or knock rummy. In the semi-deserted store, I tolerated my noisy cousins, joining them in devouring the homemade desserts—crunchy apple strudel, golden sponge cake, prune hamantaschen, and spicy honey cake. I tried to memorize their texture and taste until the next holiday.

Those sparsely spaced feasts were comic relief to our daily fare, but lessons, nonetheless, that life could be enjoyed. So today, decades later, with my mother long gone, her immutable lessons still brand me, but I have found respites of my own. My home-cooked dinners rarely deviate from a green vegetable, a starch, and a protein, but much more varied and seasoned than during my child-hood—and never mackerel! I hardly ever drink liquids during meals—except blessed wine with company—or indulge in junk food, though I'm a sucker for chocolate. And I still love eating out—*really* eating out, my nearest relative 3,000 miles away—but now gentle conversation is nourishment too.

My mother's relentless regulations—not only about food—have had their emotional consequences, but at least I have her to thank for my good health and well-preserved looks. But whenever I finish a meal and look down at my plate—whether at home or at a restaurant, alone or with friends—I'm always surprised. There they are, a mouthful of each food staring at me, reminding me that she's still here.

Estelle Jelinek has published academic articles, reportage, poetry, fiction, and, most recently, creative nonfiction, which has appeared in *The Oakland Tribune*, *The Berkeley Insider*, and *convolvulus*. After earning her Ph.D., she edited the first collection of essays on women's autobiographies, *Women's Autobiography: Essays in Criticism* (1980), and in 1986 authored the groundbreaking *The Tradition of Women's Autobiography: From Antiquity to the Present.*

"My Mother's Eating Lessons" is one vignette from Ms. Jelinek's autobiography-in-progress.

WHEN PREACHER CAME TO SUPPER

We have this family habit, coming from Papa's side, God rest his soul, of getting at things a mite too late. Not like always being late for things like school or church and such, or big things like weddings or funerals, though Granpa Norton was late to his own burial. That wasn't his fault, him being dead, but because the new undertaker took the wrong turn with the hearse after the rest of us had parked down the hill from the grave so's not to clog up the road in case someone wanted to go by during the service.

Mostly we have this way of talking about doing things until it's too late to do them the way we had thought to. Like the time Mama and Aunt Minnie invited the new assistant preacher to Saturday night supper. I'll never forget that time, especially because I'd already made up my mind to marry him as soon as I got old enough, but I reckoned for a while when we were eating supper that night that he would never want to have much to do with our family again.

When he knocked on the front door, I was the only one dressed enough, except for my beads, to let him in, though Mama did come out, keeping her back to him so's he couldn't see her dress wasn't fastened in the rear. He probably did notice she was still in her house slippers and her stockings rolled around her ankles because she hadn't fastened them to her garters yet. I felt my cheeks burning as she showed the new preacher into the parlor, then turned to scoot upstairs, her underslip and brassiere showing from the back. He never said a word, but I saw his cheeks were a bit red too. I just hoped he hadn't heard Aunt Minnie calling Mama to come help her fasten her corset.

By the time Mama came back down with Aunt Minnie, both of them were all put together, except Aunt Minnie's magenta lipstick went almost up to her nose on one side so she looked lopsided when she smiled. The preacher had been trying to talk with Granpa Chester, who was sitting in his platform rocker as usual. Trouble with talking with Granpa Chester was that he was always going to sleep, and you never knew if he heard you. He'd drop off when he was talking, too, which made it right hard to talk sense with him. We didn't much try, but the preacher couldn't know that yet. He looked some relieved when he saw Mama and Aunt Minnie, and he sprang right out of his chair to shake Aunt Minnie's hand. I couldn't help noticing how fine he looked—more like someone I'd seen in the movies than a preacher. Of course, he was only assistant, but everybody knew Reverend Hatcher was on his last legs. His sermons had got to sound a lot like Granpa Chester talking, and he'd stopped being able to scare anyone into coming down and laying their sins at the altar. I could picture the new preacher when it was his time to take over. I already knew he had a fine deep voice, from hearing him singing in the choir. So far he'd only preached one sermon when Reverend Hatcher took sick, but he was good, and he had the prettiest blue eyes.

Now that they were properly dressed, Aunt Minnie and Mama simpered around him, scolding me that I hadn't made him sit in the good chair, then sending me to the kitchen to fetch the lemonade. When I came back, he was insisting that we call him Harold. I wasn't sure I could do that quite yet, without giving away that I was already sweet on him, but I liked to spill his lemonade when I heard him say it. Mama and Minnie kept giggling and asking him personal questions until Mama all of a sudden jumped up and let out this little scream. The preacher must have thought she'd taken a spell or seen a mouse, because he practically jumped over the coffee table to get to her. I think he was flustered when Mama said she'd forgotten the roast. Then she gave Aunt Minnie a look, and the two of them bustled to the kitchen.

Next thing we could hear pots banging and cupboard doors slamming and above all that the two of them arguing if turnips was vegetable enough or should they have beans too. Mama yelled if Aunt Minnie had got out the watermelon pickles, and Aunt Minnie, all righteous like, said she was seeing to the mashed potatoes. They were talking loud at each other and making such a do I feared I should get to the kitchen. Preacher had given up trying to talk to Granpa, and sat there looking anxious. I saw Aunt Minnie come from the kitchen into the dining room and take down Granpa's Maxfield Parrish painting of half-naked women and hang up her framed picture of Clark Gable. She called me then to set the table. I was relieved to have something to do, though I did like to look at the preacher.

Finally we were all set at the table except Granpa Chester who we couldn't wake up. I think preacher worried that he might have passed on, but as soon as Granpa started snoring again, preacher got right at his supper. He was real gentlemanly, telling Mama and Aunt Minnie how good the roast and everything looked, and he only coughed a little bit when Aunt Minnie announced it was still blood cold in the middle. He let Mama pile steaming soupy mashed potatoes alongside his slice of beef and still hard turnips. Aunt Minnie rushed into the kitchen and back again with a wisp of carrot top she tucked into the potatoes, apologizing that she hadn't got out to the garden to get parsley.

No one ate much, but Mama and Aunt Minnie ran off at the mouth and told preacher their whole life story all the while he just kept chewing and chewing on his roast beef. When it was time for dessert, Aunt Minnie remembered she hadn't frosted the cake, but preacher claimed he liked his plain anyhow. When he was telling us his goodnights and thanking everyone for the hospitality, Mama pressed a big slab of the roast into hands. It was already bleeding through the napkin, but Mama ignored that. I was still that embarrassed I was glad to see him leaving. He thanked us again, and shook hands all around like preachers do. When he shook mine, he gave me a big wink, and I was some melty over that. Mama, Aunt Minnie, and I stood on the front stoop watching him walk off. By the middle of the block he had two of the neighbors' dogs following him. I would have stood watching him longer, but Mama suddenly remembered she'd left the green beans cooking. We all rushed to the kitchen, but Mama got there first and had already got the baking soda to put the fire out.

It was a good spell before I graduated high school and preacher started courting me, but it didn't take long to get at the marrying because we'd both had it in mind for a long time. I worried a bit after Reverend Hatcher died that Harold might go ahead and marry someone else, but he said it never entered his mind.

Everyone said our wedding was just about the prettiest one there had ever been in the church. Clara Pottle the organist said it was a picture of simplicity. I never knew if she meant that a little mean because Mama never did get the flowers ordered, and all we had on the altar were the left over Easter Lilies, or because Harold and I didn't dress all fancy. There was no use telling her that was because Aunt Minnie was still working on my wedding gown. None of that really mattered since the important thing was that I married my Harold.

It was too bad that we'd forgot to bring Uncle Chester to the church, but by the time we were halfway through the reception back at home, he was thinking he'd been with us all through the ceremony. When Harold and I were ready to drive off for our honeymoon, Mama and Aunt Minnie got folks together so they could throw rice at us. I had forgot to buy rice, but that didn't faze Mama a bit. Everyone threw dried navy beans at us, and they made a nice sound against Harold's new car as we drove off.

June Brown has lived in New England since 1964, where she had a long career as a group therapist/counselor for families of Alzheimer's disease victims. During that period, she contributed to two books on Alzheimer's disease. Her fiction has appeared in *Yankee Magazine*, *The Undertoad*, and *North Shore Magazine*.

"'Preacher' may have sprung from tales my Texas parents spun. For inspiration and support, I attend a local writing group, and write haiku for relaxation."

RAMPION SEASON

Wild leek fever infects
the healthy mountaineer
after snows have melted
and caps cover kettles
in the sugaring shed
when in secret places
cut by sun through ice
green spears top satin shanks
fairly bulging with sharp
promise of pungent taste
for Grampa's ramp salad,
poor man's asparagus.

BLOOD SUGAR

I. Blood

Kimberley knew she'd feel better once she got the thing out of her neck. She'd done it before and it was really easy; she always carried a pair of really sharp scissors in her backpack, just in case, really really thin scissors she slipped like a bookmark into whatever Bronte novel she was carrying around. Because Kimberley knew what they do to you, once you've passed out and can't do anything to stop them: they put this tube into the big vein on the right side of your neck and they stitch it in. Two big ugly black stitches holding down a pale blue tube. The stitches make the skin on your neck all puffy and red and, really, the whole thing is disgusting. And then, of course, they do what they're always trying to do, feed you. They run pure sugar straight into your veins. They fucking feed you this shit, without your consent, without you having to open your mouth, even. It's rape, that's what it is, and Kimberley would never stand for it.

But this time, when she'd first woken up in her pink-curtained bed, she'd felt nice. The light was all rosy and she felt warm and floaty and safe. But then she found the thing in her neck and that was the end of that. Christ. It wasn't rosy in here, it was all bloody red. It was another goddamn womb, that's what it was and they'd stuck this fake umbilical thing right in her neck. Jesus.

She sat up and reached for her backpack, fumbling around until she found it in the cheesy metal bedside table. She pulled her scissors out of *Agnes Grey* and smiled: they were really so dumb, all of them. If it was her, and she was going to force-feed some poor schmuck of a girl, she'd be smart enough to take away the girl's backpack, at least. God, they were lame.

Kimberley could do it without even looking in a mirror but since there was a little flip-up one in the tray table, she went ahead and used it. Actually, she kind of liked to watch herself get the thing out of her flesh.

II. Water

The stitches made neat little snapping sounds when she cut them: ping, ping. And then the tube thing could slide right out, simple. You just exerted a nice steady pressure and, zip, out it came. Kimberley always thought she wouldn't look at it afterwards: the nasty thing was always longer than she'd imagined and it made her dizzy to think how it had been inside her, without her permission. And it was always still leaking a gross sticky liquid: sugar water. But she did look before she dropped it on the floor and pressed her finger to the spot on her neck where the blood was welling up. Then she closed her eyes and leaned back on her pillows, satisfied.

III. Sugar

The face that appeared in the crack of the curtains was fat and hideous, its mouth open, its red hair sticking out in all directions. "Jesus, Mary and Joseph," it said. "You've got blood running all down your neck, girl. What are you, some kind of vampire or something?"

The face was splotched with freckles and its mouth was missing teeth. Kimberley looked at it for one minute and then she shut her eyes again. She hated roommates. Really: she'd had some weirdos.

The curtains opened farther and the whole fat girl came into

Kimberley's side of the room. Kimberley could smell her—sweaty, with greasy hair. She sighed and opened her eyes.

The girl grinned. "Shitfire, child, you are the skinniest human I've ever seen. Pure bone. Is that from being sick, or what?"

Kimberley sat up. "I'm not sick." She folded her hands on the sheet, neatly. "What's wrong with you?" Hell, she might as well ask; she knew the roommate would tell her anyway. They always do.

The girl plumped herself down on the end of the bed. Kimberley folded her legs up, quick, so her feet wouldn't touch the fat girl. "My sugar's real high. I'm a diabetic and I keep passing out. And I'm way pregnant, you know? So they say I got to be real careful. With my other kids, I was OK, but this one, shit, it's like to kill me." She put a fat hand on her fat belly.

IV. Salt

"You have kids?" Kimberley looked hard at the girl. "How old are you?"

"Seventeen. I got twins, boys, they're almost two. Holy terrors. How old are you?"

"Sixteen." Kimberley couldn't stop staring. The girl still had pimples, for God sake, sore red spots all mixed up with her freckles. Pimples and twins. It wasn't right.

"Yeah? You look a lot older, skinny and wrinkly as you are. You sure you ain't sick?"

"I'm fine. I just fainted, that's all. Everybody always overreacts. It's nothing, really."

"If you say so. You want your breakfast? They brought it an hour ago and you ain't touched it. They're starving me."

Kimberley looked at the tray sitting on the chair at the foot of her bed. She'd been smelling it, right along, she realized. That was what was making her feel so awful. She shook her head. "You can have it."

"All of it?" The girl's eyes lit up. "You don't want nothing?"

"Take it," Kimberley said. She felt the weight lift off her bed when the fat girl stood up. She straightened her legs out. "Wait," she said, before the girl disappeared through the curtain. "Just give me the little salt thing, OK?"

The girl turned, the tray in her hands. "That's what you want? This little thing?" She held up the tiny red and white packet. "You got pancakes here and cereal and scrambled egg and juice and coffee and this is all you want?"

Kimberley nodded. "That's what I want, yes."

The girl shook her head and handed it over. Then she lumbered to her own bed and sat down with Kimberley's tray, clearly happy.

Kimberley snapped the packet open with one quick flick—it came apart nicely, straight on the dotted line. Then she touched her tongue gently to the salty slit and sucked.

V. Milk

And so, after all the yelling and bullshit with the nurses when they came in and found the thing out of her neck, and after all the same kind of yelling and bullshit when they figured out that LeeAnne, the fat girl, had eaten all those foods she shouldn't, things settled down. Kimberley promised she'd eat something later and LeeAnne took more insulin and they watched reruns of "Gilligan's Island," on their separate TVs, and laughed at the same stupid lines.

And the day wore on and the light inside the pink curtains was really OK, Kimberley decided, and she slept. There were orders from her doctor that her parents couldn't visit her, so that was all right, and, really, she was feeling better. LeeAnne ate both of their lunches and dinners, and both girls swore to the nurses that Kimberley had eaten her own, so that was OK, too. This whole thing, actually, was turning out OK, all around.

So when LeeAnne gave a sharp little scream, sometime in the night, Kimberley got right out of bed and went to LeeAnne's side of the curtain. In the hospital half-light, she could see LeeAnne sitting up in bed, looking down at her fat pale legs. The legs were spread apart. LeeAnne looked up at Kimberley. "Shit, man. It was just a dream," she said. "I was dreaming about when I had the twins and it hurt. Then I thought I was losing this one." She took one last look between her thighs, then laughed and lay back. "But I guess not."

The nightgown over LeeAnne's loose breasts looked sticky and wet. Kimberley pointed. "What's that all over you?"

LeeAnne looked down at her chest. "Oh, jeez. That's just milk, girl. I been nursing the twins and then I got pregnant again and it just never stops."

Kimberley reached out farther and touched the spreading spot on LeeAnne's chest. "Milk?"

"Milk. I got enough for ten kids, I swear. Look." LeeAnne reached down and pinched a nipple. A stream of liquid soaked her gown.

Kimberley's hand squeezed the wet cotton. Then she lifted her hand away and tightened it into a fist. "You'll stay a few days, won't you, LeeAnne?" she whispered. "Maybe we can stay here together and be roommates and just, you know, rest?"

But LeeAnne was already sighing into sleep and she didn't answer.

Kimberley climbed back into her own bed, pulled the pink curtains tight, and put her fist into her mouth. It was unbearably, terribly, wonderfully sweet.

Hollis Seamon is the author of *Body Work*, a collection of short stories (Spring Harbor Press, 2000). Her stories have also appeared in *Chicago Review, The American Voice, CALYX, The Hudson Review,* and *13th Moon*. Ms. Seamon teaches writing and literature at the College of Saint Rose in Albany, New York.

"Once, in Babies Hospital in New York City, I was on a floor with a group of teenage girls who were starving to death—fierce anorexics, hunger artists supreme. Many of these girls were reading novels by the Bronte sisters; the novels matched the girls—strange, brilliant, ravenous, and angry. Twenty years later, those girls and their books still haunt my dreams. 'Blood Sugar' comes from them."

LET THEM EAT CAKE

"Commander Garpitok, what did you do to get this remote assignment? It must make your optical sensors leak to keep watch over a nothing ball of gases and an infantile species."

The commander narrowed three of his eyes at the ensign, measuring the youth: he was brash, impatient, though still a good navigator. There was much the commander would have to teach him. "Ensign," he sighed out of his lower mouth, the top one narrating the distinct sequence of codes keyed to the coordinates of their assignment into the mouthpiece extending from the smooth faced console. A seemingly random pattern of lights in different colors flashed and pulsed in response to each utterance. Finished, the commander breathed deeply, settling comfortably back in his pod. This was a familiar trip to him. Soon it would be for the ensign as well.

Perhaps the boy would come to enjoy the solitude of this lonely stretch of cosmos and the diversion of the amusing creatures on the cloudy jewel of a planet, as he had. If not, it would teach the boy to be more careful in his choices for the mating rituals. The admiral was still fuming over the ensign's boldness with his second son.

Garpitok chuckled into the mouthpiece, causing the console to bleep its confusion. He reinstated the technical portion of his mind to the task of automation and regarded the ensign, amusement sparkling in his left eyes.

"Ensign, this nothing ball of gases and infants may surprise you.

120

This species, though poorly developed, has an impressive amount of potential. Unlike our race, their prime intelligence has two distinct species. What they call Man and Wo-man. There seems to be a great amount of discord between the two, though in general they are amicable."

"Who is the ruling class?"

"Often the men. And in some population groupings, by women much like them."

The ensign scanned his memory banks for examples, then nodded.

Garpitok continued. "They seem to value a separate type of power overall. Women are trained to be the more decorated of the species, though at times it is hard to be sure. They put much effort into conforming to generalized images of acceptable beauty. The men accept this as their role and encourage its upkeep. It helps keep the Wo-men's interference in the system controllable."

"I take it the Wo-men are an amusement construct of little intelligence or ability."

"On the contrary, Ensign. This Wo-man contingent is bright and has great intuitive powers. They are the ones we were first in contact with hundreds of thousands of their earth time ago. Over what they call centuries. Airdentains," he clarified, prompted by the ensign's look of confusion. "Since our last direct contact, Men and Wo-men have switched and forgotten their former roles. It makes for some fascinating observations."

"But if they were in power, what is to stop them from taking it again? And why have they not? And what is the point of us watching them for airdentains when they have progressed so pitifully?"

The commander patted the ensign's nearest appendage. He understood the youth's annoyance at the seeming futility of standing guard over the planet that was just now coming into view on the screen.

"Ensign. If Man and Wo-man ever learn to combine and utilize

121

their strengths in concert, their development would undergo an evolutionary explosion. They would then have the potential to become a power in this galaxy and in time an influential voice on the intergalactic counsel."

The ensign looked dubiously at the cloudy blue ball on the view screen, his outermost eyes drooping with doubt. "Then how," he continued softly, "have they been so off track for so long?"

The commander waved several tentacled extensions over various parts of the console, a knowing smile on both mouths. The view screen blurred then slowly focused. "Perhaps it would be easiest to show you."

The screen flickered. An outdoor restaurant appeared, its tables covered by white tablecloths, set with crystal and china, gold accented silverware and linen napkins. The restaurant was crowded with mostly women sipping spritzers, fruity creations, or creamy concoctions with umbrellas. Men and women in black dress pants and white short coats hustled from table to table stationed around the main runway, hurrying to get in the bulk of the orders before the two o'clock fashion show began.

The screen focused on a table of five women seated just to the left of the runway. A petite brunette stared at the menu, clucking softly to herself. "Everything here is so rich. Maybe I should just get a salad."

"Julianne, are you on another diet?" the woman to her right, dressed in a white suit, with carefully sculpted hair, asked distractedly.

Julianne laughed sheepishly. "I'm not sure if it's another one or the reincarnation of a past one."

"You know what they say," chimed in a third, swearing under her breath at the chip in her precisely manicured nail. "Same shit, different diet."

"Isn't that the truth," the fourth agreed. "Personally, Julianne, I don't see why you need to diet. You look perfectly lovely."

"That's what I thought," she nodded deprecatingly. "Until I went bathing suit shopping last week."

A silent "ah" of recognition rippled through them.

The commander turned to the ensign. "Have you had a chance to witness the bathing suit ritual?"

"No, Sir. What is it?"

The commander smiled. "A yearly pilgrimage women like these make to their commerce centers. They go for several sessions to battle with stretchy scraps of material. They carry them into rooms with single compartments and single reflecting surfaces with a separate three-angled one outside where they can elicit input from others. Or they go into large rooms with reflection surfaces all around. The lights here are bright and cast good shadows on any protruding piece of flesh, allowing for proper self-castigation. They rarely speak to each other, unless to point out the faults of the bodies they've chosen." He glanced at the ensign to be sure the youth was still following his explanation. "The point of this ritual is to gain confirmation that their chosen bodies are poor and hopelessly flawed for the costumes selected, and therefore *unfit*. It is quite amusing." Garpitok chuckled at the memories playing across his personal view screen.

"But why would they submit to such treatment? Who forces them to do this?" interrupted the ensign.

"No one forces them. It's a type of self-measuring process they choose to see how far from the societal ideal they are."

"Why don't they just change the ideal or throw it out completely?"

The commander shook his head indulgently. "My dear Ensign, you've much to learn. Perhaps we should continue observing."

A waiter stood beside the table, pad and pencil ready, a white cloth folded neatly over one arm. "And for you, Ma'am?"

Yvonne stiffened at the term and tightened her smile. "I'll have the chicken cordon bleu and the arugala salad with blue cheese dressing. On the side." Her smile warmed at her blatant disregard for both the cholesterol and calories.

"Very good, ladies. I'll be back promptly with your hors d'eouvres."

The other women eyed Yvonne admiringly in his wake. "I am splurging," she stated nonplussed. "I've earned this." In her mind, she calculated the miles she'd have to do on her stationary bike to compensate for her bravado, but she held her head high.

The ensign extended his two center eyes nearer to the screen, as if a closer look would decipher the scene.

"Sustenance on this planet is like a dance," the commander explained. "It is comfort they run to, torture they run from. Or it is torture they run to, comfort they run from." He scratched his head with a forked tentacle. "They use it to soothe themselves, to punish, cajole, protect and isolate themselves." The commander snorted. "They seem to use it for everything but sustenance itself."

"I don't understand," the ensign broke in. "It is sustenance. We consume as celebration of continued prosperity and life."

"At times they do this," the commander agreed. "Mostly," he sighed dismissively, "it's a dance. Back and forth, with no point or progress."

The ensign shook his head and returned his attention to the screen.

The women were chatting over their meals. "Have you tried that kick-boxing class with Tanya?" Yvonne asked, barely dipping the tines of her fork into the dressing before spearing a chunk of lettuce.

"Did I ever," murmured Elaine, nibbling carefully on skinless chicken and steamed vegetables. Inwardly, she fumed about the mishap with the car door handle. Another fifty-dollar touch-up, she thought grimly, frowning at her hand as she tried to hide the offending digit. "I'm still sore."

A wispy model floated past them in an airy tank top of silk and a matching miniskirt fluttering a third of the way down her slender thighs.

Marlene lit a cigarette, careful not to get any ashes on her white suit. "Would you look at that," she marveled acidly as the model moved out of earshot. "My legs weren't that skinny when I was born."

"I could donkey kick and liposuck until doomsday and I would *still* not fit into that outfit," sighed Kathleen.

"Oh, I could," quipped Yvonne.

The other women did a slow take of their companion.

"Yes," she smiled cheekily. "It would fit my left leg perfectly."

They laughed, the sound losing some flight as the next slim figure approached. A slinky blonde with incredibly long legs draped in clingy fabric from shoulder to toe glided towards them. Marlene pushed her plate away and tapped her cigarette box, preparing the replacement for the one dangling from her deep red lips.

"Marlene, I thought you'd given those up," Kathleen observed gently.

"I know the drill," she replied crisply. "They age you, they wrinkle you, they kill you." She motioned to the blonde. "I'm already older and more wrinkled than the competition. At least I have the satisfaction of helping the process along." She glared at the young woman, searching diligently for flaws and comparisons.

The waiter was a welcomed interruption.

"Coffee, ladies?"

A sigh of relief echoed silently around the table.

The fashion show complete, a waiter came round with the dessert tray. The ladies murmured wistful sighs of, "I'd like to. I wish I could," and sad dismissals of, "I shouldn't, I couldn't, I can't."

"Is this what these Wo-men do?" asked the ensign incredulously. "Compete with each other, eat, mourning every bite, while deprecating themselves? I don't understand. There is such a range of diversity among them. How can this be a problem?"

"Their diversity is only a problem because their societal agreement is that it is one."

"But you said this race is promising. How can such a backward, confused society be a potential universal influence? Are these the lowest denominators you show me? Are these women lacking in intellect, skill and worth beyond their outward packaging?"

"Of course not, Ensign," the commander huffed, put off by the suggestion that he might have chosen poor examples for them to observe. "These women are well-educated, well-spoken." His upper mouth uttered a syllable and the screen focused on Marlene's carefully made-up face. "This one, for instance, was a brilliant debater in her educational years. She was persuasive and compelling in her arguments. When she spoke, people listened. Old ideas were challenged. She has the makings of a great legislator for the rights of their underprivileged."

Another command, and Yvonne's hard-edged blondeness swiveled into view. "This one was a diligent protestor for change when she was young. She carried signs and staged peaceful protests, bringing social problems to the public's attention.

"And this one." The screen focused on Julianne. "She is a great teacher. She has a gift for inspiring her students to explore their talents and abilities. She could help revolutionize their present confining, controlling system of education and make it serve all better, especially the young.

"This one has great healing abilities," he pointed to Elaine's face with a forked tentacle. "She has a heart that hears the messages beyond the symptoms of her patients. Current constrictions in their system prevents her from fully using those gifts, however."

"And the last one?" asked the ensign.

Kathleen's face shimmied before them. The commander uttered three syllables and the image steadied.

"She has great gifts for working with animals. She would be an asset in healing the rift between these Hu-mans and what they call the lower species of their planet, benefiting all life here."

"Then why do they not?" The ensign focused all eyes on his commander, eager for relief from this puzzlement.

"It is their construct of society. The separate camps, Man and Wo-man, tacitly agree to keep the obstacles in place in their systems so that they do not disturb what they call the status quo. For some it is the present benefit they see for themselves, not realizing in the end they'll lose out for it. For others it is comfort. Change is fearful for these creatures. The familiar, even if scarcely bearable, *feels* safer to them. It is what they know. For still others it is helplessness and worthlessness. They feel they don't deserve better or couldn't have it if they tried. They feel that they alone are not enough."

"But you just said these five women here could make great changes. What if they banded together? What if they cast off their current system and focused their collective powers?"

A broad smile broke across both of the commander's mouths. The wheels were turning in the ensign's head. He might do well at this yet. "Yes. Indeed. What if?" He turned his attention back to the view screen. "That is why we are here, Ensign."

Julianne sighed, putting down her coffee cup. "Have you ever wondered what we could do if we took all the energy and money we spend talking about food, exercising it off, dieting, trying to look right and be right? Have you ever wondered what we could do?"

A spark flickered and flared in each woman's eyes. "Imagine the research we could do," murmured Marlene.

"The policy changes," sighed Yvonne.

"The advancements in healing and treatment," murmured Elaine wistfully.

"And education," Julianne added dreamily.

"And the environment," Kathleen put in.

A deep passion surged within each woman. Old, dormant dreams stretched stiffly, cracked open crusty, sleep-filled eyes.

"Commander, look!" the ensign gasped, pointing with several tentacles to the unfolding scene. The energy released in the awakening thoughts of each woman fanned the fire in the others. "There is real hope here. If they can combine their talents, draw strength from each other, they could ignite hope in others. They could begin the revolution that advances this planet after so many airdentains." The youth bounced in his pod, breathless, unable to contain himself. "What do we do now, Commander? What? What do we do?"

"Control yourself, Ensign," the commander snapped, focusing all his attention on the task ahead. "I have everything under control." The view on the screen widened. The commander uttered a guttural string of commands. The screen focused on the retreating head of the waiter with the dessert tray. A pinpoint light flashed behind his ear. He waved at it as if it were a stinging insect. Then he turned around carefully, and headed towards the table of women still lost in their bubbling reveries.

Another series of commands, and the plates on the tray glowed momentarily.

"Watch," the commander breathed, resting back in his own pod.

"Ladies, can I offer you dessert today?" the waiter gestured to his display.

The women turned, eyes glazed with dreams of possibility, to look at him. "No we already…" Yvonne's voice trailed off. The gooey confections of chocolate, creams, raspberry and pastries seemed to hum and sing to each woman.

Their mouths watered.

"Let's go for it," Kathleen whispered conspiratorially. "Let's all be *bad*," she stressed gleefully. The dreamy fire was replaced with wicked gleams as each woman chose a different dessert, each feeling a rebel's vindication.

"I'll have to pedal ten extra miles every day for a week," giggled Yvonne.

"So much for a new bathing suit this year," sighed Julianne wistfully.

"Hey, let me try a bite of that double chocolate mocha torte,

Elaine." Marlene reached across the table with her fork.

"This is heavenly," Kathleen murmured, eyes fluttering closed as she savored her marble cheesecake with fresh raspberry sauce. "You've all got to try this."

"And this cherry Black Forest cake, too," added Marlene, moving her plate to the middle of the table.

The women gathered closer around the food, reveling outwardly in their perceived decadence. Inside, each silently mourned the extra workouts and the moment of truth waiting in their bathroom mirrors.

The watching aliens could almost see the women's stirring dreams roll over, curl up, and settle unnoticed back to sleep.

The ensign sighed heavily, slumping back in his pod, relieved, exhausted. This assignment was going to be more challenging than he'd thought.

"What shall we do, you ask, Ensign?" The commander proudly flashed bright rows of copper-colored teeth. "Let them eat cake."

Anne Tremblay is a writer from Massachusetts, with work recently appearing in the Bloodreams publication, *Creative Cauldron II*, and their on-line Ezine by the same name, *Voices*, and non-fiction appearing in *Our Times*, *New Woman*, *The Merrimack Journal*, and the upcoming book, *Secrets of Super Star Speakers*, among many others. She is currently working on a collection of short stories, a series of young adult fiction, and her latest novel, *Beautiful*.

"Let Them Eat Cake" was born during a time spent preparing for a workshop called "Food, Self, and Mirrors," where Ms. Tremblay was reflecting on our country's obsession with how we look and how we think we should. "What if," she wondered, "this whole obsession thing wasn't of our creation, but was merely a manipulation of other beings who's sole purpose was to keep us running in helpless circles?"

ROSE HIP PUREE

Pear-shaped cylinders, prickly red,
Festoon the quiescent bushes.
Haunting fragrance accompanies
the harvesting of gaudy bells.

De-blossom, boil, and press the fruit.
Boil and press again, and sweeten
With nectar's yield, amber honey
Stored in full combs while roses bloomed.

Spread on hot potato biscuits
Or eat for dessert like a sauce.
Seal some into sterilized jars
For a winter taste of summer.

And when your country roses bloom,
Even though they lack perfume,
You'll anticipate the harvest boon,
Of rose hip puree with tea.

INGREDIENTS

The bell rings. Knuckles tap at the door. Mother opens it and I stand behind her. Stepfather, Larry, is in the basement changing a light bulb.

Merry Christmas! Hello, hello! Kissy, kissy comes toward us from Uncle Leon and Aunt Mary.

Their daughter Annie poises herself behind them with a blank face, her pale hands clutching a black patent-leather purse. Her little blonde curls fall around the collar of her long, dyed-pink rabbit coat.

Pink in the winter, I exclaim privately as I drop my head down toward my red satin dress.

Annie walks past me without a word, locked alone in her 12-year-old world with no time for an eight-year-old cousin. Step-cousin at that!

Uncle Leon carries three shopping bags full of presents to the living room. I follow. He stands there with his arms stretched out not knowing what to do since the tree already spills packages half way into the room.

Annie situates herself at the edge of the sofa. Her arms wrap around that small patent-leather bag as if she expects gypsies to jump out and snatch it.

Mother ushers Aunt Mary into the kitchen where she insists her sweet potatoes must be admitted to a warm oven or else. Or else what, I wonder.

The door bell rings. More knocks. Mother rushes from the kitchen leaving Aunt Mary talking. I rush to be with Mother. This time it is Aunt Louise and her husband, Dick. Aunt Lydia and Uncle Bob are there, too.

Aunt Lydia's little Patrick, the youngest of the cousins, now five, weaves in and out of the adults, slides between his sister Carolyn and Aunt Louise's Cathy. Past Mother. He pauses in front of me and kicks my leg.

Ow, I yell but no one notices because they watch and laugh at Aunt Louise's Gary, who ought to know better at 13, as he charges after Patrick and is the cause of the chase.

Gary stops in front of me, presses his lips against mine, worms his tongue to open my mouth then my teeth then thrusts it down my throat. I think it will reach my bellybutton. I gag and get away from him.

He and Patrick run downstairs to the basement.

Stepfather emerges from the top of the basement steps. Merry Christmas, he shouts. He grabs shoulders, shakes hands, hugs, pats heads.

Merry Christmas, he says to Grandpa. I look up to see little Grandpa who must have come in one of the last cars. Under his right arm, he carries an open box containing the food he will eat tonight. A twin box rests against his left hip and carries the collection of photos and letters he has received from extended-family members throughout the year.

Diane, Mother says to me, take these loaves of bread from Aunt Louise.

I stretch my arms straight to accept the long loaves of French and Italian bread that I identify only because that is what is printed on the wrappers of each. Aunt Louise and Uncle Dick are neither French nor Italian. They don't even cook. They eat out or bring in.

I follow Mother, who carries a bowl of green beans and another containing a leafy salad. Mother had accepted them from Lydia, who hardly said hello before she rushed, arm in arm with Louise, to the living room to share secrets. I watch Mother set the bowls on the counter. She stands there and I want to ask if she is okay but I don't. The door bell rings and I follow her like a little duckling.

Mother opens the door to find little Johnny standing there. Uncle Lance and Aunt Jo plus Vickie and Margaret are getting out of their car down the street. Johnny runs by us to the basement door. Mother waits without a word. I wait with her.

Carolyn and Cathy appear from the living room from behind me and say, can we play with your dolls?

I say yes and they run toward the back of the house to my bedroom.

Merry Christmas, Virginia, Jo says to Mother, gives her a kiss and pins a beautiful corsage on her dress.

Hello Diane, she says to me.

Vickie, my favorite cousin, six years older than me, stands at her mother's side. I wait in between visits for Vickie so we can play canasta.

She always wins but I learn tricks from her so I can beat my friends.

Vickie carries a large tray mounded with cookies.

I made all of these, she says to me.

They look good, I say. I made the Jell-O salad for dinner, I say to her, all by myself. She looks at me as if to say Jell-O making is for babies.

It's not regular Jell-O salad, I say. It has bunches of ingredients in it like cottage cheese, canned milk, nuts, olives. Lots of stuff. It's complicated to make.

Mother and Jo talk quietly in the kitchen corner while unpacking more potatoes and the cranberry sauce. Jo is Mother's only confidant in the family.

Margaret joins Annie on the sofa. They sit and talk softly with an occasional giggle.

Vickie and I go to the basement to play cards. The boys are angry because they cannot play ping pong. The table is set with silver, china and goblets at twenty places. Vickie and I sit on the floor and she shuffles the double deck of cards. Patrick starts to come toward us and changes his mind. Vickie is older than all of the boy cousins and they don't cross her.

Gary would never put his tongue in her mouth.

Uncle Lance's voice carries from the top of the stairs. He wants us up for the annual photo shoot. When we come into the room, Stepfather stands with a brother and sister on each of his sides: Lance, Louise, Larry, Lydia, Leon. They scrunch into one mass as if creating a fantastic new mammal, arms tightly stretched and wrapped with hands clutching another body where they can.

Stepfather says something that only the other four can hear and they convulse into laughter. Uncle Dick, one of the five spouses that the real family members call out-laws, asks what is so funny. No one pays any attention to him. Uncle Bob takes the photo: focus, click, flash.

Another one, yells Stepfather, but with Dad in it this time. They break free, add little Grandpa to the middle and huddle once again. He stands alert and proud of his children.

Vickie and I stand together and watch as Stepfather calls for the out-laws. Grandpa walks to us and says to Vickie, who is your little friend? I look around the room. I look at Grandpa, at Vickie, at the room.

The uncles become bright blue carousel horses, the aunts bright pink. The merry-go-round begins to move, slow enough for the cousins to jump on. It spins faster. Then faster. I watch this step-family that I've known since I was six months old streak into some other form. I look down at my hand and realize that I hold the brass ring.

Grandpa says to me, give me that.

Vickie looks at Grandpa and then at me. She turns back to

Grandpa and says, Grandpa, this is Larry's stepdaughter, Diane. Grandpa looks at me, smiles and walks away. Vickie looks at me and we both turn to watch the adults.

Come on, all you out-laws, Larry says for the second time to the spouses of his brothers and sisters, to his own spouse, my mother, who is nowhere in sight.

Virginia, he yells and then she appears from the kitchen.

There they are lined up: Uncle Bob, Aunt Jo, Mother, Aunt Mary, Uncle Dick. They don't wrap their arms around one another. No hug. They don't touch. Uncle Leon says, cheese, they smile: focus, click, flash and they disband as quickly as they can, having been in this family photo quite by chance of having married who they did. Imagine if they had married other people and had gone tonight to other parties, different people here in their place, people we don't know, will never know.

I move to sit on the three-legged stool. Uncle Lance mans the camera this time. Okay, he says, now the cousins.

Vickie, Margaret and Johnny are the first to obey their father's command. They stand rocket tall in front of the fireplace. Annie joins next.

Come on Patrick, Gary, over here. Where are Carolyn and Cathy?

At that moment they come from the hallway, each with two of my dolls. Carolyn carries my favorites, Sally and Polly, by the hair and Cathy trails behind carrying Susie and Samantha by their feet. I want to punch them right in their arms. No that's not true. I want to smash my dolls in my cousins' faces.

I wonder where I will stand in the photo.

Uncle Lance says, cheese! Focus, click, flash and it is all over. I sit on the three-legged stool.

Stepfather comes from the kitchen and says, dinner is ready.

I carry my Jell-O salad to the basement, to the ping-pong table set with red and green poinsettia tablecloths. Down the stairs we go. Everyone is sitting at the table when I get there. I move from one to the other and say, here is my Jell-O salad. I made it myself.

Patrick says to Aunt Lydia, Mommy that looks yucky. I don't want any, I want Vickie's cookies.

That's all right dear, says Aunt Lydia to Patrick.

I dance from person to person. I hold the bowl of Jell-O salad like a waiter in a fancy restaurant, on top of my open flat hand that faces the ceiling. I do a cartwheel and perch the bowl on top of my flat foot as it stretches into the air. The family passes Aunt Mary's sweet potatoes and Aunt Louise's French and Italian breads and Aunt Jo's cranberry sauce and Mother's turkey. Vickie's cookies decorate the middle of the table.

I jump onto the table taking care to not upset my bowl of Jell-O salad.

I skip in and out of plates, cranberries, baskets of bread. I pass my bowl under the nose of each, one by one. No one notices me.

It is forty-eight years later, Christmas Eve on Long Island with our house, Gustavo's and mine, bulging with our six shared adult children and their partners. Gustavo sits at the kitchen table with pages of white paper spread out, each with names at their tops. This morning we each carry out a particular task toward the preparation of tonight's dinner.

Okay, he says to Carlos and his live-in companion, Nancy, the turkey has defrosted in the refrigerator for three days. All you have to do is take it out and follow the directions printed on the bag.

I take their photo, the three, and capture Carlos saying, but Dad, we've never done this before.

Yes I know, Gustavo says, and that why it's your turn. You will prepare the best, most succulent turkey in the world and will have gained the confidence to do it again whenever you want to.

Yeah, yeah, says Carlos with good nature, teach a kid to cook a turkey rather than cooking it for him and for a lifetime he knows how to do it.

Edourd and his Italian wife, Rita, enter through the front door. We have the wine, they announce, everything you asked for, Dad.

I turn with my camera: focus, click, flash.

I take a bottle out of the case, wine from San Gimignano. Another from Sonoma, from Mendosa and from Burgundy. I know that Gustavo has sent them with the list of wines from places we've visited, places about which we have some of our fondest travel memories. I nod at Gustavo and he smiles back.

My older son, Paul, stands at the stove and puts fragrant spices into the simmering sugar-water mix. He adds a bottle of red to make the mull that we will sip from now until dinner. The others, except for Gustavo, huddle around him also to take a whiff. Focus, click, flash.

My younger son James, his girlfriend Karin and Gustavo's daughter Rosa come from upstairs ready to peel potatoes and make desserts. They each take a glass of hot wine just as Paul's new wife, Yoko, comes through the front door with an armload of sunflowers. It's her first Christmas in the U.S.

Where did you find these gorgeous things, I ask in amazement considering the snow I see outside and the temperature in the teens. Focus, click, flash.

Maria and her partner, Jennifer, and Rosa's live-in boyfriend, Gary, set the table with perfection.

Yoko says, where should I set these flowers?

In the middle, says Jennifer and now I know why they decided on the yellow tablecloth rather than the red. Focus, click, flash.

I set the camera down. I weave in and out of the potato peelers, the dough roller, the wine stirrer, around the five now sitting at the kitchen table humoring Gustavo about his lists.

The tea kettle whistles. I measure two cups of boiling water into a bowl where I have already placed the contents of two Jell-O packages, one lemon and one lime, and mix until dissolved, integrated, interfused.

I set the mixture aside to cool and blend a pound of cottage cheese with a cup of mayonnaise and one six-ounce can of evaporated milk. Onto this I scatter one eight-ounce can of crushed pineapple.

I set this blend aside and chop the stuffed green olives from a small jar along with a half-cup of walnuts. I add all ingredients together with a pinch of salt. Stir, mix. Lumps among the smooth.

Later when we sit to eat I move the wondrous sunflowers to the sideboard so we can see one another. I set the Jell-O salad in their place to remind me about the ingredients of life combined to blend the similar, the odd, the step, and real into new unions, into a family that takes everyone into consideration.

We toast, we eat, we talk and laugh. We represent two generations, four countries: different languages, cultures, customs, and values.

After dinner I call everyone to the couch for a photo. We sit on the couch, on the floor, stand in back. I focus, set the timer and run to be included: flash!

———

Pam Burris, born and educated in southern California, is a writer on Long Island as well as an administrator at SUNY, Stony Brook. She has previously published in the Papier-Mache Press anthology, *At Our Core: Women Writing about Power* and small literary magazines. She is currently working on a novel about a large physics department on the north shore of Long Island that hires its first woman physicist.

BARBECUE

Beef and pork. Forget chicken. What you want here is fat spicy links and tender ribs. Truly barbecued. In a brick oven. A deep, almost gruesome one, very hot and smelling of charred flesh. Better if a very large man with no shirt is tending the fire and serving the orders. He will ask you how hot you want your sauce to be, and grin knowingly when you confidently order the very hottest. Do not hesitate. You want the most fierce they've got, the kind the men pride themselves on eating. Order a combination plate, too much meat for even such a large man as him. Hope that he reaches into the furthest recess and pulls out portions that have cooked for a long, hot, smoky time. He will ladle black red sauce onto the paper plate and silently give you an extra slice or two of white bread. He believes he is being kind. Don't bother to eat it. Take all the fixings. Slaw, not macaroni. And a slice of sweet potato pie which you will take home with you afterwards and also never eat.

Company is important. Take along a friend who likes to eat. Who loves to eat. Not someone fastidious or delicate, save those people for crepes. You want company that understands the Paleolithic urge, hedonism riding the edge of gluttony. Also someone who drinks. Stop to purchase a pint or two of dark ale, the kind that tastes like the blood you suck when you rip your cuticle. The kind best served warm. One of you will cradle it between your thighs on the way. The other must hold the dangerously stacked plates in their lap. Take turns a little too quickly. Let some of the sauce seep through the brown paper bag. Never mind the napkins.

There should be a deserted wharf, or a ramshackle pier. One with large posts grown fuzzy and gray, faintly reeking of dead marine life and urine. One where old men fish for nothing but time.

A windy day is most suitable. You want the soft lapping of white caps, your hair ruffled, your voice carried off some distance. Walk far enough out that your car looks small. Far enough out to leave teenagers and anglers behind. Find a bit of wharf somewhat free of sea gull droppings, where both of you can lean against the pilings and speak out over the waves.

Disregard the plastic forks, they are for amateurs. Lick sauce from your fingers as you take out the soggy, dripping plates. Hold them folded on your lap, balanced in one hand. Feast like a Viking with the other. Let the heat of it make your eyes stream tears and burn your lips. Wipe them with the back of a fist. This is as close as it gets.

CHOCOLATE

Dark chocolate, bitter and brittle. Almost Baker's chocolate, those paper wrapped squares of children's disappointment, "How come they smell so good and taste so bad?" Then, we don't understand sweets without sugar, the alchemy of heat and milk. Try to get yours from a confectioner who will shatter large, craggy chunks with a small silver hammer. Think about soldiers offering Red Cross bars to children.

You need an umbrella. A large, black, canopied one. Go to an antique shop, a dusty collectibles. It must be an old umbrella, with a polished wooden handle turned up in a hook, with sturdy stays and an inch-long steel tip. The kind Dickens' gentlemen tapped on cobblestone. The fabric should be heavy, musty canvas. Buy some black rubbers while you are out, or a too large pair of galoshes. Ones with long rows of tin snaps. No zippers. Wear either over comfortable shoes. Wear an oil cloth slicker if you have one, banana yellow plastic if you don't.

Wait for a rainy night. Not a thunderous downpour with gusting torrents, but a steady rhythmic summer's rain, soaking the ground, running down gutters and pavement in shallow ripples. You need an old college campus. Or a private school. An ancient collection of brick towers and rambling pathways. Wait, too, for late night, as dark as the chocolate itself outside the golden haze of the twisted iron lampposts. Late enough for you to encounter only the occasional diligent lab student or a few laughing couples with newspaper held over their heads.

Stuff the chocolate into your pocket and step out into the night. Open your umbrella and carry it tilted forward, as though you were braving a squall. Nibble small bits as you splash through each puddle until the chocolate is gone and you are soaked to the knees. Home again, you may sip strong black tea, piping hot.

Toni Amato has appeared as a guest speaker/performer at Brandeis, Temple, and Goddard Universities, and participated in "Homogenius," and "Bodies Edge," two multi-artist installations at Temple University. She received a Vermont Studio Center residency to work on her current novel, *Nobody Rides For Free*. Her work has been published in several anthologies, including *Our Voices* (Joan Nestle, editor).

"Food magazines and cookbooks have always been my personal choice of erotic reading... and will someone please make publishers never, ever again let there be cookbooks without glossy pictures? The way one eats, the company, the setting; gourmets have long written of the importance of these things. I wanted to speak to the less *fancy*, perhaps, but still deeply sensuous experiences of food."

EAT THAT

"Eat that," Daddy said, pointing at the salmon patty.

Friday night was fish night. The worst. Tiny boned, canned salmon mixed with cornmeal and hunks of onion slapped into circles. They were fried black on the outside, but still raw on the inside.

That's what Momma had fixed on that hot night in 1957. The June evening I came to think of as my family's Last Supper—the beginning of our long crucifixion.

I poked at the orange stringy stuff with a fork, hoping by some miracle it would disappear.

"Teresa, listen to your father and eat." Momma backed up what Daddy had said. But that was nothing new. That's what she always did. It was her job.

I looked at my sister, Nadine, chomping away, her rosy cheeks all aglow, her healthy skin clear and creamy. I wanted to reach across the gray Formica table and whack her—I really did. But I was ten and too big to pull a stunt like that.

Nadine dabbed her lips with a napkin and shoved her empty plate away. Then she polished off a huge glass of milk. She was a good eater and not just because she was sixteen. She'd always been a good eater. I had always been a bad eater. Maybe our good-girl/bad-girl split had started with our eating habits, but now the split had carried over into our very beings. She was sweet, and I was surly. She got good grades, and I got bad grades. She obeyed, and I disobeyed. She prayed, and I played.

Everybody loved Nadine, even the meanest nuns, even a surly little sister like me. You couldn't help but love her. She was always looking out for the other guy and went out of her way to do good deeds while trying to keep them a secret. And plenty of times she had saved me from Daddy's wrath.

While Nadine was still gulping her milk, Daddy flipped open the Kansas City Star and hid behind the headline: "Khrushchev Attempts to Lull West."

"I've got povatica. You want some?" Momma asked.

Nadine nodded. She always said yes to food, especially Polish nut bread.

I was amazed Nadine wasn't a fatso, but she wasn't. She had a gorgeous shape. Joey Lomiski, one of the many boys who had a crush on her, called her 'stacked.' When I asked her what that meant, she blushed and said I shouldn't listen to any of those Lomiski boys.

"Can I take it to my room, Momma? Nadine asked, buttering a thick slice of povatica. "I've got to get ready for my date."

Daddy crinkled the paper, smashing the Joe Palooka comic I'd been reading on the back page. "You're not going on any date to-night. Your mother and I have a date."

Nadine's head swung back to look at Momma. Momma was smiling, something she didn't do that much. She was pretty when she smiled, and Nadine was lucky she took after her. I favored Daddy, the same dishwater blond hair, the same hazel eyes, the same long nose. Momma and Nadine had thick, wavy chestnut hair, big green eyes, and cute little noses.

"But Momma," Nadine said. "We're going to the drive-in."

"Drive-in!" Daddy hollered. "With who?"

"A boy I met at C.Y.O. Momma's met him. He's..."

"You told her she could go to that passion-pit, Margaret?" Daddy turned a hard look at Momma.

She stopped smiling. "Take it easy, Ross. Nadine's a good girl."

Momma was always trying to get Daddy to take it easy. Most of the time he didn't listen. I sat up straight and waited to see if he got that crazy look in his eyes. If he did, look out. He could go on a long rampage, sometimes at Momma, but mostly at me and Nadine. He'd cuss and holler and call us names. He'd say he was going to kick out our lungs, beat us to a bloody pulp or kill us where we sat because he was our father and he had the right. And sometimes he'd use the belt on us—well on me, because Nadine was a good girl and didn't need a whipping the way I did.

Still, his rages scared Nadine, too, and she grabbed the table like she was getting ready to watch a tornado touch the ground. Momma frowned and scooted forward in case she had to jump up and shut the windows. She worried the neighbors might hear the commotion.

"Daddy, please," Nadine begged.

"You heard me. You're staying with your sister. And I don't want any boys in this house while we're out."

"I promised. I want to go so bad."

I was getting worried. Nadine didn't usually provoke Daddy once he'd said no.

"What about what your mother wants!" Daddy yelled. "Do you ever think about that?"

Nadine started to cry before Daddy even finished his sentence.

"Let her go. We can go another night," Momma said in the calm voice she used when she was trying to keep the peace.

Daddy slapped the newspaper against the edge of the table. "Selfish tramps, that's what you want to raise!"

I jumped an inch off my chair. Nadine stopped crying. She looked like she'd stopped breathing.

Momma was on her feet, tugging at the window.

"Forget going out," she said, lowering the window with a thump. "I don't care if we never go out."

Everything got quiet. I'd never heard Momma talk back to

Daddy—ever.

That was worse than the yelling, waiting during the hush for the hitting to start. Not that I'd ever seen Daddy hit Momma, but right now that didn't mean much.

BAM! Daddy slammed his fist against the table. The dishes rattled as if the earth had moved. "I said we're going out. And, by God, we're going!"

All of a sudden Daddy stopped looking at Momma and leaned toward me. "And you eat that." His eyes were bright and the vein on his forehead bulged green and ugly. I'd seen that lizard vein before. Anything could happen when that lizard vein came out.

"If Teresa eats, then the son of a bitch can pack both of you off to the goddamned drive-in."

The legs of Daddy's chair scraped against the floor as he stood up and got right in Nadine's face. She tried to back away, but she was trapped.

"Go on and go. Act like trash. See where it gets you."

Nadine flinched as if Daddy had hit her. A second later he stormed out of the kitchen.

Nobody moved.

The corners of Momma's mouth turned down and a far-off expression crossed her face.

Nadine was frowning and she looked angry and sad and hurt all at the same time.

I was pretty happy. I had already started imagining going on a date with my sister—to the drive-in. Wow! What did I care if I was trash? I couldn't worry about that with a movie at stake.

Momma got up and filled the sink.

Nadine started clearing the table. Her hands were shaking. "You heard what he said," she snapped.

I looked down at the smashed patty swimming in a puddle of grease and pretended to stick my finger down my throat. Barf!

Nadine gave me a dirty look.

I ate. Forced down two nasty bites anyway. After that even the thought of the drive-in couldn't get that third fork full anywhere near my mouth.

Nadine finished stacking the plates and slipped me a dishrag. I slid my food into the rag and watched with amazement as she stuffed the whole mess under her blouse.

Momma turned around looking like she knew something was fishy. But all she said was, "Go get your rosaries."

We had started saying the rosary after supper ever since Bishop Sheen had announced on his TV program, "The family that prays together stays together." Momma propped her picture of Mother Perpetual Help against the pink lamp on the living room drum-table and the three of us knelt in a circle. Daddy got to say his rosary from the Lay-Z-Boy because he'd been on his feet all day at General Motors where he was boss.

"In the name of the Father, and of the Son, and of the Holy Ghost," Daddy started out and sounded so downhearted I looked over at him. I couldn't stand the thought of him being sad, and, as mad as I'd been at him at the supper table, now I felt sorry for him. I decided I'd offer up my rosary to St. Jude—the patron saint of the hopeless cases—that someday Daddy would stop acting like a wild man.

It took a long time to say the rosary. "Blessed is the fruit of thy womb..." What would be playing at the drive-in? "Holy Mary, Mother of God..." A double feature with werewolves and vampires? Wouldn't that be the living end! "Pray for us sinners now and at the hour of our death..."

Amen. Finally. I blessed myself in a hurry and made a beeline for my bedroom. I tore through my closet looking for my favorite pedal pushers and matching sleeveless aqua top.

Just as I'd finished dressing, Daddy came into my room. "You mind your sister tonight."

I promised.

He leaned down and kissed the top of my head. "I love you, Punkey."

Ever since I was little and couldn't say pumpkin he had called me Punkey.

"I love you too, Daddy," I answered and meant it.

"Do what Nadine tells you," he added again, handing me a shining half-dollar.

The minute the folks backed our red Rambler out of the garage, I rushed into Nadine's room. She was standing at the foot of her bed wearing a white half-slip and a strapless brassiere. She crossed her arms over her chest. "Why do you always barge in here?"

"Do not!" I sassed, but the look on her face made me say I was sorry real quick.

"Thank God," she said, yanking a spaghetti-strapped yellow dress over her head, "this time next year I'll be on my way to college or modeling in New York City."

"Uh-Uh!" I hollered louder than I had planned. Before I knew it my cheeks were wet. Nobody was more surprised than me. I'm no crybaby. I didn't cry when Eddy Beach socked me in the stomach or when Sister Clovis pounded my knuckles with a ruler. But what Nadine said was true and the thought of losing her hurt me like nothing else, not even Daddy's whippings. The truth was, Nadine already had a scholarship to college and she was a model. Sort of a model. She'd been chosen Miss Auto Show last fall and got to pick the winning ticket for a new Edsel out of a fish bowl while reporters snapped her picture.

Nadine sat on the stool in front of her dresser. "Don't cry," she said reaching out and hugging me. "We're going to have fun tonight." She let go and looked at me. "And you'll always get to irritate me. You're my baby sister, aren't you?"

I nodded and took the hankie she handed me. Mopping my face, I sat on the edge of her bed and watched her line up cold cream, lipstick, mascara and pancake makeup. Before long we heard a car with a loud muffler pull up in front of the house.

"That's Chris!" she said, getting all excited.

I hurried to the window to take a gander at Mister Dreamboat. "Chris is a girl's name."

"It's short for Christopher, silly."

A red and white '56 Ford stopped in front of our house. I had learned a lot about cars when Nadine was Miss Auto Show.

"Hot stuff! A two-toned convertible!"

"Shh," Nadine said, smiling. "He'll think you've never ridden in a car before." She pulled me away from the window and pushed me toward the living room. "Go let him in. And act like a lady."

"Since when do ladies have any fun?" I mumbled on my way to the living room.

Through the picture window I watched a tall skinny guy barrel up our steps two at time. His head was down, and he ran his fingers through his black hair like he was James Dean or something.

"Good evening," he said through the screen door. "Chris Marquell, here to collect Miss Nadine Malovich."

Collect? Miss Malovich? What a weirdo. I opened the door and he stepped inside.

"Tell her I'm here." He had this deep clear voice like a radio announcer that made everything he said sound important.

"Please be seated, Mister Marquell," I said all stiff and formal to mock the way he talked, but I don't think he got the joke.

"I'll stand," he said looking down at Momma's new sectional. The sofa was the same aqua color as my pedal pushers, only it had these cool little silver flecks all through it.

"Suit yourself, but Miss Malovich could be awhile. She's putting on her face."

He made a big deal about sliding back the cuff of his long-sleeved white shirt and looking at his watch. After that he stood in front of the picture window and stuffed his hands into the pockets of his black trousers. I figured he must be roasting in that getup, but when he lifted his arm to do that thing with his hair again, I didn't see any sweat.

"I'm Teresa," I said, taking a peak outside to see for myself what was so fascinating. I didn't see anything unusual—the Beal kids riding trikes, and Mr. Krebs pulling up dandelions in the twilight.

"The kid sister," he said, and kept staring out the window.

"Older. I'm seventeen."

That got him to look me in the eye. "Very funny."

His eyes were an icy blue with lashes almost as long as the fake ones they sold at Woolworth's. And you'd think a guy with a convertible would have a suntan, but his skin was nearly as white as his shirt.

"You go to school with Nadine?"

"High school? Hardly."

I wasn't born yesterday. I could see he was an old guy, twenty-four or twenty-five, maybe. I just wanted to see what he would say. "I get to go on your date tonight," I said, smoothing the front of my shirt.

"You think so, do you."

"Know so."

Nadine walked in squinting at me the way Sister Clovis used to do when I made her really mad. Sister Clovis would've boxed Chris' ears if she'd seen the way he was looking Nadine up and down. He whistled and said, "Nice."

Little red dots came into Nadine's cheeks. She put her arm around my shoulder. "You've met Teresa."

"I've had the honor," he said, still gawking at Nadine. "You ready?"

"She's a bit of pistol, but she grows on you."

You could tell he didn't believe it.

"I have to watch T. tonight," Nadine explained. "Do you mind if we take her along?"

"Of course I mind," he said, pausing long enough for Nadine to get nervous. "But if you say so, darling."

Darling! Where did he get off calling my sister *darling*. I figured she'd put him in his place. Instead she smiled and swiveled out the door like Loretta Young on her TV show.

I tried to squeeze in next to my sister, but Chris said, "Back seat."

As we drove away, I sat on my knees to make myself taller and hoped Cindy Kelso, my ex-best friend, would be out in her yard. I wanted the whole neighborhood to see me and Nadine cruising along in such a flashy car.

I hated our neighborhood. We'd lived here a year, the sorriest year of my life. The kids were a bunch of stuck-up snots. The girls wouldn't play with me unless they were mad at their other friends. If they did play with me, they wanted to do something dumb like dress-up in old clothes, wear popbeads and earrings and wobble around in high heels. What fun was that? These kids didn't know how to have adventures. In my old neighborhood, a gang of us would walk to the corner store, eat fudgesicles, and make fun of people getting on and off the streetcar. Or we'd sneak down to the dump where we weren't supposed to go and look for treasure. For a fact, the dump was stinky and you might stir up the rats, but that was part of the excitement. Around here there weren't any stores to walk to, or streetcars, or dumps, and everybody stayed in their air-conditioned ranch houses, even the kids. But Momma kept saying this was a good neighborhood and we ought to thank God we'd moved up in the world, away from all those people from the Old Country.

When we rounded the corner in front of Cindy's house, I yelled, "Kelso!" thinking I could get her to come to the window.

Chris tilted his head and stuck his finger in his ear.

Nadine turned around and lightly smacked me on the leg. "What are you screaming about?"

Chris' cold blue eyes caught me in the rearview mirror. "There'd better not be any shoes on my upholstery."

"There's not," I lied, chalking up another sin for Confession. Then I slipped off my Keds and enjoyed the rush of the world going by and the night wind whirling around my head. My hair kept flying into my mouth, but I couldn't help smiling; not until we stopped at a red light and I noticed Chris drawing little circles with his finger on Nadine's naked shoulder. When he shoved his finger under the strap of her sundress, I wanted to grab that filthy digit and crack it backwards.

Instead I stuck my head in between Chris and Nadine. "Why'd the moron throw the clock out the window?"

No answer.

"He wanted to see time fly!" I said, slapping Nadine on the back. "Mommy, Mommy, why am I running around in circles?" I inched forward. "Shut up or I'll nail your other foot to the floor!"

"Those are so awful," Nadine said, but she was smiling. Chris didn't smile. He didn't know a good joke when he'd heard one. All he did was tug on his shirt collar before the light turned green.

"I know a bunch more shut-up jokes," I offered.

"I think we've heard enough," Nadine said. "And don't breathe down Chris' neck."

"Did you hear the one about the..."

"Sit back until we get there. I mean it, T."

"All right already!" I stretched out in the back seat, squeezed my eyes shut, and pretended I'd been kidnapped by bad guys. I'd have to tell the police where the mugs had taken me even though I was blindfolded. That was easy when Chris drove over the viaduct and I got my first whiff of the stockyards. "Phew," I said, thinking of the one bad thing about a convertible—you couldn't roll up the windows to keep out rotten smells.

Once we were over the bridge and past the stink, I stopped holding my nose, opened my eyes, and watched the clouds float over the moon.

We turned a sharp corner and I bounced against the seat as the car jolted over two sets of railroad tracks. I sat up just in time to spot the big orange and green neon sign flashing a white arrow toward the Boulevard drive-in.

"Forgive the unattractive atmosphere," Chris said, pulling out his billfold, "but this is the only place showing *The Wayward Bus*."

"Jayne Mansfield! A dirty movie!" I said. "Banned by the Legion of Decency."

"It is not," Nadine said.

Chris laughed and stopped in front of the ticket booth and handed a Mexican lady two dollars. She didn't say a word and waved us through. Chris drove down a narrow paved road with little lights on both sides, then onto a gravel path in between rows of steel poles holding up speakers. He parked in the next-to-last row.

A clock with top hats for numbers and a black walking stick for a second hand ticked away on one side of the movie screen. TEN MINUTES TO SHOW TIME flashed beside the clock in red letters. Hickory burgers, corn dogs, popcorn and soft drinks complete with legs in fishnet stockings tap-danced and kicked high toward the audience. Another message below the toes of the dancing food read: GET YOUR TASTY SNACKS AND DELICIOUS SOFT DRINKS AT THE CONCESSION STAND.

"You need binoculars from way back here," I griped.

"What do you care? You'll be watching the movie from the concession," Chris said, putting the top up on the convertible.

The concession stand was a small cinder block building plunked in the middle of the drive-in. It looked about a mile away, and had a patio with lawn chairs and speakers for anybody who didn't want to watch the movie from their car.

Family cars, boxy Buicks, Oldsmobiles and mostly station wagons were parked close to the food or way down front next to the swing sets right underneath the screen. The hot rods and cool cars were parked in the back rows.

Chris mounted the speaker on the driver's side and "Rock Around

The Clock" crackled into the car.

"I'm dying for a hickory burger," I said. "I don't care if it is Friday." Before I even had to think about spending the fifty cents Daddy had given me, and committing a sin, Chris waved a dollar bill in front of me. "Here," he said. "Get whatever you want. Just eat it down there."

A whole buck. "Gee, thanks." I snatched the bill out of his hand before he could change his mind. "You guys want me to bring you anything? Ah, later I mean."

I should've saved my breath. They were too busy making goo-goo eyes at each other to answer.

I wiggled out of the back seat. "Don't look for me anytime soon. I'll probably run into some of my own crowd down there."

"Wait." Nadine started to get out of the car. "I'll walk with you so you'll know how to find us."

Chris grabbed her arm. "Stay here! She's not helpless!"

Nadine pulled away. "I hate being yelled at."

"I'm sorry, angel," he said, in a hurry. "Blame it on the half-pint sister."

When we were a little ways from the car I kicked gravel. "Hells Bells. I wish that were my convertible. I'd make him thumb his way home."

"Don't cuss," Nadine said, grabbing my hand as we walked between the rows.

We passed two people who had spread a blanket on the hood of their car and were leaning against the windshield.

"Chris has had a hard life," Nadine said. "His Momma died when he was younger than you. And his father left him in the orphanage with the Sisters in Quebec."

"Too bad if he had to bunk in with the nuns, but that doesn't mean he has to act like such a smart aleck."

"Why do I try to explain anything to you?"

We had reached the back of the concession stand where the toilets were. They didn't smell as bad as the stockyards, but almost.

The line of women and kids waiting to use the bathrooms stretched halfway around the building. I got behind two teenagers who wore identical red short-shorts and exchanged puffs off the same cigarette. The taller one had skinny, suntanned legs.

"You going to be okay?" Nadine asked me.

I rolled my eyes.

"All right. Stay out of trouble."

I watched Nadine walk away, and so did all the guys who passed within fifty feet of her.

"Sure is filthy around here," I said to the girls in front of me to strike up a conversation.

The tall girl looked at me over her shoulder. "Who pulled your chain," she said, causing her sidekick to double over giggling.

I decided I didn't have to go that bad and went around front and flopped into one of the lawn chairs. There were lots of chairs, all of them empty. The clock on the screen blinked: THREE MINUTES TO SHOW TIME. People hurried back to their cars carrying little paper trays piled with food and drinks. Everybody walked in twos or fours or big groups. I could smell the popcorn and the sweet barbecue for the hickory burgers, but I'd lost my appetite. I was busy picking at a scab on my elbow when I heard a familiar voice.

"Why the sad sack?"

"Say, Joey. You're a sight for sore eyes."

Joey Lomiski was a short blond kid with a sweet round face. He was from my old neighborhood and his grin reminded me of all the people I missed. Six Eskimo pies built a little pyramid in his paper tray.

"How'd you get caught in this den of sin all by your lonesome?"

"I'm with my sister."

He kept grinning and looking around.

"Don't have a cow, Joey. She's with a date."

"Who's the lucky devil?"

155

"He's a devil all right. I wish she was here with you."

"Ditto, Kiddo."

"A guy named Chris Marquell."

"Marquell? " Joey said, frowning.

Behind him, the clock disappeared and the food high-kicked off the screen. A sweep of red letters announced: COMING ATTRAC- TIONS. Lots of Indians were being gunned down by guys wearing ten-gallon hats.

"I hope that ain't the same Marquell my brother knows. What's he look like?"

I looked back at Joey. "Tall and skinny. Black hair not in a duck- tail, but almost, and he dresses funny."

"And he's from Canada? Talks funny too, real formal like?"

"Is Quebec in Canada?"

Joey nodded.

"So what about him?"

"I don't know if I should tell you."

"Come on, Joey!"

He looked down at the Eskimo pies. "Hate to tell you kid, but that guy's got a wife and baby up there. I know for a fact."

I stared at him for maybe two seconds before I jumped up and started running. I could hear him calling after me, but I kept on going. I ran all the way back to the car, but skidded to a stop when I saw the screen flicker and Chris kissing my sister.

Nadine's head was pinned against the seat and Chris' mouth moved over her face and down her neck. Disgusting!

I went around on Nadine's side and panted, "I gotta tell you something!"

They pulled apart fast.

Chris slumped behind the wheel. "Jesus."

Nadine turned real white. "You all right?"

I nodded, trying to catch my breath. "I ran into Joey Lomiski down there. You know, Joey Lomiski."

"Pipe down!" a guy bellowed in the next car.

"Get in," Chris ordered.

I climbed into the back seat. "He's adultery," I blurted out, pointing at Chris. "Joey said…"

I was drowned out by the roar of the motor. Bugs Bunny's cute face filled the screen, but I only got to see him take one bite out of his carrot. The Ford was flying past the other cars and blowing up gravel. The speaker cord had snapped away from the pole and Chris heaved the box out the window. It twirled along the ground, but Chris didn't even look.

"What's *wrong*?" Nadine asked, staring at Chris.

"We'll talk when we're alone," Chris said as the tires squealed on the paved road that led back to the viaduct.

"Joey said…" that was as far as I got when Chris half turned around. "Shut up, or I'll slam your teeth down your throat."

"What's the matter with you!" Nadine said, shocked. "Don't talk to her like that. She's just a kid."

Nobody said anything after that.

We were home in a hurry. The house was dark. It was too early for Momma and Daddy to be home.

Nadine turned on the light and said I should stay in my room and get ready for bed.

Mister Adultery followed her downstairs to the rumpus room. I put on my nightgown and crouched down to listen at the closed door. Chris was doing all the talking, but I couldn't make out the words. After I got a charley horse in my leg, I gave up on hearing anything juicy and hit the hay.

The next morning, Momma and Daddy were off doing their usual Saturday morning grocery shopping. Nadine was drinking coffee alone at the kitchen table. She looked awful. Traces of mascara streaked her cheeks and her eyes were red and swollen.

"So, did he confess?" I asked, proud that I had gotten the goods on Chris. "He's adultery, isn't he?"

"Will you stop saying that," she said in a flat voice. "People are adulterers, not adultery."

She looked so miserable I didn't have the heart to ask her if she was going to fix breakfast. Nadine always made us pancakes or French toast on Saturday mornings. It was the only meal I looked forward to.

"Anyway, it doesn't matter what he is," she said, staring off into space. "I'm never going to see him again." Then she looked me in eye. "Don't ever tell Momma or Daddy. You hear?"

I crossed my heart and hoped to die. Then I climbed on a chair and got down a box of Frosted Flakes. I offered Nadine a bowl— but she said she couldn't eat.

The rest of the summer I didn't see much of my sister. During the day she worked at Woolworth's and at night she stayed in her room studying for college exams. I kept my fingers crossed she'd have another date and take me along, but she never did.

One morning after school term started, Momma told me to hurry Nadine to the table.

"Why do I bother to cook. Now both of you eat like birds," Momma said, whipping eggs in a bowl.

Through the locked bathroom door I heard Nadine heaving. "Momma wants you," I shouted, "but I'll tell her you're sick."

She opened the door a crack. "No! Don't tell," Nadine said. "I'll be out in a minute." She had such a scared look on her face, I got scared too, and ran to tell Momma that Nadine was throwing up.

A week later I came home from school and heard all kinds of racket coming from Nadine's room. Daddy was throwing Nadine's stuff into boxes. Her closet was already bare and he was working on her desk. He had that mad look in his eyes worse than ever.

It was risky to say anything, but I had to know. "What happened to Nadine? Where's my sister?"

He kept pitching books and old stacks of *Modern Screen* into a box. "You don't have a sister anymore," he said. His voice was low and dangerous. "And don't you ever mention her name in this house again."

I ran to my room, fell on the bed and screamed, "Nadine. Nadine," over and over into my pillow.

Daddy kept his word and pretended I didn't have a sister. Momma went along, but I could hear her crying late at night.

Two days later Momma sat me down on the sofa. "If anyone asks, say your sister moved to Florida to take care of your sick Aunt Shirley."

"What's wrong with Aunt Shirley?"

"Nothing. Just say what I told you."

"But that's a lie."

Momma shot up and jerked me up too. "You obey me for once!" she yelled, squeezing my arm. She looked like she was going to cry. "Get out of my sight," she said.

Three weeks later I was so lonesome I hung around Cindy Kelso's yard trying to get the courage to ring her doorbell. Just as I was walking away, she came outside with two new girls from the neighborhood.

"Teresa," she called. I smiled and came up to the porch thinking she was going to introduce me to the new girls. They were brown-eyed towheaded twins that looked like a pair of bookends. I was having a great time staring at them. But when Cindy whined, "so your sister's gone and got herself knocked up," I looked away from the twins and faced Cindy's big fat smirk.

I didn't know what *knocked up* meant, but I could tell by her singsong voice and the way the twins snickered that it wasn't anything good. I was thinking Nadine might be in jail, getting it mixed up with *locked up*.

Cindy swept her hand in a big half circle over her belly. "Everybody knows Nadine's in one of those homes for unwed mothers."

First I kicked her in the shins. Then I dived on her, yanking her long brown hair with one hand and pinching her meaty arm with the other. She squealed and begged for help, but the twins stayed wide-eyed and frozen. Cindy started swinging. I ducked while hanging onto her hair even when her fist smacked me square in the eye. Boy, that hurt, but I kept jerking on that stringy mop of hers. I only let go when Mrs. Kelso came outside and screamed, "What in the world!"

I raced home and was almost there before I noticed the strands of hair locked in my fist.

Momma was frying salmon patties. Daddy was drinking a Pabst Blue Ribbon at the kitchen table.

"God in heaven," Momma said, putting down her spatula. "What happened?"

"Cindy Kelso hit me."

"You let that butterball give you a shiner?" Daddy said. "You can't fight any better than that?"

"Oh, for God's sake," Momma said, leaning down and looking at my eye. "You want her to be a street fighter."

Daddy didn't get a chance to answer before Momma went on, "Why did she hit you?"

"I pulled her hair."

"Why?"

There wasn't anyway I could say it—knocked up. How could I say that about my sister?

"Answer your mother," Daddy threatened.

The patties sizzled in the frying pan.

"If you won't tell me," Momma said, getting a tray of ice from the freezer, "then go to bed and don't expect any supper."

I walked to my room holding the ice bag over my eye. Poor me. No salmon patty.

I didn't want to believe it, but the pieces all fit—I knew what that dog turd Cindy Kelso said was true. But months passed before I had the guts to ask Momma, "Is Nadine still in that home for unwed mothers?"

She was peeling potatoes at the sink, and gouged the knife down hard and didn't look at me. I thought she'd deny it. Instead she said, "Not anymore. Not since she ran off with that Chris character and shacked up with him like a common... The shame she's brought on this family. The disgrace!" Momma's words rumbled on like a runaway train. "She's lost. She's living in sin. And your father's disowned her, and that's the end of it."

The end of it?

I hated my parents. I hated my neighbors. I hated my God. They had all turned against Nadine. Most of all I hated myself because Nadine hated me, too. She hadn't said good-bye. She hadn't sent a note. Why wouldn't she hate a little snitch like me? I was the one who'd told Momma that day she'd been throwing up. And I was the one who'd blabbed that night at the drive-in. It was all my fault.

On the outside everything looked pretty much the same, except we didn't pray after supper anymore and the house was awful quiet. And I was in even more trouble than usual. At school almost everyday I fought with some loudmouth for calling Nadine a whore or a tramp or a slut. But before long, I was the one picking fights with whoever happened to be around. That was good, I thought. That was better than wrestling with my own torn heart.

Seven months later my parents said we were going to see Nadine. She was in the hospital. We drove forever to get to this podunk Kansas town that didn't even have a stoplight.

Behind the desk in the hospital lobby, a sourpuss with thick glasses and a pinched nose told us where Nadine's room was. "She'll have to stay here though," the sourpuss nodded at me. "No visitors under fourteen."

"NO!"

Momma took me to the other side of the empty room. "T., We have to follow the rules."

"NO!"

Daddy came over and whispered, "Maybe we can sneak you up after awhile."

I watched them take the elevator upstairs. A half hour later, when the coast was clear, I snuck up to Nadine's room on my own.

I came up the back stairway and saw Momma and Daddy walking down the hall toward the elevator. Their backs were to me so I couldn't see what they looked like. But Momma's head was low, and she jerked away from Daddy when he tried to touch her.

Chris was sitting in a chair next to Nadine's bed. He looked the same, only his hair was a little longer. But my sister didn't look like anyone I knew. She was tiny and sunken with big eyes staring out like the starving Jews I'd seen in Life magazine.

Chris stood up when he saw me.

"T!" my sister said and held out her arm, a stick of an arm so skinny I was half scared to touch her.

"The kid sister," Chris said.

I wanted to kill him so bad it must've showed because then he said, "I'd better make myself scarce again."

On his way out he pointed to my sister's food tray. "You'd better eat that."

"It doesn't look too bad," I said, after Chris was gone. "Maybe you should eat."

"I can't," she groaned. "Please take it away and come sit by me." I carried the tray across the room and came back to her. She patted the bed and I sat down.

She looked so different! Her teeth were gray, her skin was pasty, her hair was dull. The only sign of the old Nadine were her eyes and even they weren't the same—too glassy and too bright.

"Do you still hate me?" I asked, regretting later that my first question had been about me.

"Hate you? I could never hate you."

"You never said good-bye. You never wrote."

"I was too ashamed," she said, looking away from me. "I'm still ashamed."

I had no answer to that. And forever after I regretted the things I hadn't said: she shouldn't be ashamed, she shouldn't starve herself, she should live and be happy and be the person she was meant to be.

But at the time all I did was put my head down on the stiff white hospital sheet.

After the funeral, Chris went back to Canada and asked Momma and Daddy to take Nadine's baby. He was a chubby baby with rosy cheeks and wispy black hair. His eyes were big and green. Momma sat him in a highchair across from me.

"Now remember, Teresa," she said. "He's an orphan who's come to live with us." I looked from Momma to Daddy to get his reaction. Daddy chewed his food with a dead look in his eyes.

The baby giggled and banged a cup on the tray of his highchair. Momma spooned strained carrots into his mouth. When the jar was empty she leaned toward him and whispered, "Aren't you a good little eater."

Leslie Powell is a writer, editor, and agent with Cambridge Literary Associates near Boston, Massachusetts. Her work has appeared in *Pandora, Zoetrope All Story Extra, Heartland USA* and other publications.

"The story 'Eat That' came from a mix of images and characters I knew and heard about as I was growing up. We had all heard of girls who 'got into trouble' and what became of them was often spiritually and psychologically, if not literally, a kind of death. These were the times when sex outside marriage was viewed with great shame—for the girls, anyway—and the punishment for 'getting caught' was ostracism, humiliation and often loss of their babies if they were unable or unwilling to marry. Lately, when I hear so much of 'family values' and the cry to 'bring back shame' as a cure for our social challenges, I think of these girls and the bad old days. Unfortunately, for vulnerable women and children the bad old days still exist."

YO-YO GIRL

I couldn't help falling in love with a Pillsbury salesman, though it wasn't the money or the prestige like you might think. I met Phil while temping for a food service distributor, one of those strange, secret businesses you might never know existed unless you were possessed one day with the desire to discover how processed foods get from factories to restaurants. Or you became a temp. I answered the phone and typed a few letters and tried not to get caught doodling.

Phil was out of the office most of the time, selling his Pillsbury products, but we played flirty little games on the phone every time he checked in with the boss; he taught me to recognize his voice the first week. I put as much sex into my professional greeting as I could and he always warmly said my name back to me and waited. If I said his name without prompting he'd bring me something, a calendar or a Pillsbury Doughboy in durable white rubber, or muffins he'd baked to try out new product. Who wouldn't fall for that kind of attention? I pictured mornings in bed with him and a halfdozen fresh-from-the-oven Banana Nut muffins. On rainy winter Saturday afternoons we'd curl up in front of his VCR with coffee and hot strudel sticks dripping with warm, cinnamon-spiced apple filling.

If I couldn't see him or talk to him on the phone I typed his letters passionately—they were usually concerned with innovative ways to use Pillsbury products or special offers to help sell classic items. I typed listlessly for the other sales reps. I couldn't feel the least speck of interest in *their* products. What could be less sexually stimulating than canned spaghetti sauce or chicken tenders? When I gave Phil his completed letters to sign, I blushed and held the sheets against my body so he had to step in close to take them. I wore vanilla perfume so he'd smell me and think of baking.

In a few weeks I wasn't just fantasizing about late night Pillsbury snacks and breakfast muffins. I was planning a Pillsbury wedding. We'd invent our own sophisticated little appetizer pizzas with Pillsbury's self-rising dough and fancy quiches poured into Pillsbury's ready made Flaky Pie Crust. He'd bake the wedding cake himself, spongy chocolate layers covered in rich cream cheese frosting.

Don't think I was trying to seduce and entrap a contented bach-elor. Phil wanted to get married. He was thirty-two, and he talked about "when I get married..." all the time in a generic way, as if all he needed was the right woman and everything would arrange it-self. I was determined that he at least consider me for the role. The warm and fuzzy nature of his job had me fascinated. I don't think I was alone in this attraction either. I think Phil saw my domestic potential. He needed a curvy sort of woman, a woman not afraid of food. A woman who could take his job seriously.

After a month of clandestine muffin tastes and little presents we went for a casual after-work drink. I leaned excitedly across the small bar table listening to all the Pillsbury possibilities, fabulous recipes not given on the back of the box. I wanted him to take me home and bake for me that very night. My infatuation had become an obsession and I didn't care that Phil was attractive, but nothing like the stringy athletes I usually fell for. He had thinning blond hair and dark eyes and he was a little doughy.

After the drink we progressed to movies and dinners but I was impatient. I didn't want to go out. I wanted to take a hot bath and put on a fuzzy robe and have him come over to my under-heated studio with partially-baked scones to put in my oven and I'd mix up some international coffees and sit on his lap.

Phil wanted to know all about me, about my plans, but that's why I was temping, I didn't have any. I'd had eleven jobs, eight boyfriends and six apartments in the last two years. He began to be suspicious of my fascination with his job and its perks. Pillsbury was so full of home and family associations, I decided I was drunk on stability. Our house would never be without muffin mix. With him I would never feel lost or unstable. I wondered if Pillsbury or any of its subsidiaries made baby formula.

I tried not to seem too eager but waking up in his bed one Sunday morning, far from my little apartment with its depressing green kitchen stocked with instant oatmeal and cold cereal, I felt so fulfilled it was madness. I almost fainted with completion when he asked tenderly if I was hungry, but then I nearly fell off the bed when he suggested we go out for brunch.

Oh no. Patio dining? Omelets and mimosas and sliced cantaloupe? How cold and bachelor-like. I wanted to open the can of Wild Maine Blueberries for him, leaving enough juice to stain the muffins slightly purple. To lean against him in his blue-and-white tile kitchen as they baked and puffed.

"Couldn't we fix something here and eat breakfast in bed?" I stuttered nervously. Would he guess how important this was? Once he understood the romantic potential intrinsic even to Low Fat Raisin Bran muffins he would never go back, I was sure, to crepes suzette and tossed salad with black walnut vinaigrette, but it was dangerous to let him think I only loved him for his samples. I moaned into his mouth and whispered, "Bake me some muffins, please."

"Then we wouldn't have to get dressed," I continued brightly, pulling back seductively and tying his furry blue bathrobe loosely around my waist. I lured him into the kitchen where he must have had ten different kinds of Pillsbury muffin mixes in the plain blue and white food service boxes.

"That's what you want?" he asked and I nodded but I still wasn't quite satisfied. I was dreaming of the frontier.

"Do you have anything not in stores yet? Something ... experimental?"

He was amused. "Blackberry-Lime?"

"Oh yes," I cried and he let me help stir the batter and gently lap a bit from his finger.

We put them in the oven hurriedly, both of us aroused by now. His robe slipped off my shoulders, I pushed his boxers aside, and when the oven timer buzzed, I came. The smell of crisp browned muffins filled the kitchen and we took them out and ate them steaming.

He fell in love with me for being so unmaterialistic and easy to please. I never wanted to go out for expensive dinners or to fancy concerts. I listened, absolutely absorbed, when he told me about his day. I was a little crazy, I think, but I've never been so happy. Days at work flew by and I threw myself into every bit of word processing. Maybe I'm not the first girl driven round the bend by clerical work. But that wasn't it, it was him, it was the muffins. He knew everything about those muffins, about Pillsbury. He told me stories about the founding of it, things buried in the mythology of the Head Office. He even told me a secret ingredient. I was sure I was finished with my nomadic and unfaithful ways.

Nobody ever loved him the way I did. Maybe you're thinking love isn't food and food isn't love but it was all stirred up together. I wouldn't settle for my mother's mess of a homemade kitchen, full of flours and sugars and graters and zesters and peelers. I wanted to tear open a box and find instant, eternal bliss.

My muffin man began talk about marriage to me. At first I was triumphant, but I began to worry. Would this strange passion of mine last? It had survived five whole months already but there was a hitch—I was fighting off some weight gain with long solitary walks and aerobics. However, my Pillsbury bread product intake had not slowed and I couldn't keep up. I didn't mind too much. I was happy as a soft-bellied sex pot, but it was the first sign that my cravings might have to be repressed, thus ending the free, thoughtless joy of this carbohydrate-rich affair. I was afraid that if controlled, the lust would fade.

About a month later I caught my salesman looking at another girl in the office, a slender vegan. Maybe I imagined the desire in the look but I was alarmed, and I began to scour the magazines for a crash diet that included a dozen Pillsbury products a day. No luck. It was all fruit shakes and steamed vegetables and then, too horribly fortuitously, I met a cute Odwalla delivery driver at 7-11. It was a brief light affair during which I lost 20 pounds, but I'm not sure if it wasn't due more to grief at the loss of my muffin man than to the drastic bike rides and liquid diet. Protein shakes and sugary juices occupied me for a time, but I soon longed for rich buttery kisses again. My temp job had ended soon after I betrayed my love so I couldn't even see him at the office and he ignored my pages and changed his cell phone number. I had nothing to occupy me.

I stayed with my skinny and inadequate Odwalla man a little longer but in two months my favorite jeans were falling off my hips and I definitely wanted Phil back. I felt cold and thin and unsatisfied. We could take long walks together, perhaps, and ration our love-snacks to especially romantic occasions.

I lay in wait for him one evening outside his apartment. He came home around 8 and I watched him from across the street. He still looked sad. I was wearing my tightest jeans and a clinging top so he would see my wasted body's need for him and his product.

I rang his doorbell and he let me in but stood, arms crossed over his little paunch, in the hallway. The sweet smell of his home weakened my knees and I tried everything I could think of to shred his defenses. He didn't know how he could trust me again.

"I was just afraid," I said, "I had to revisit my old life of dumb affairs and silly food fads to know for sure you were the real thing.

He was just a protein shake, something you like well enough while it's in your mouth. But you're … bread." (Or muffins, but I couldn't say that.) "Bread is life."

He almost smiled but he said, "You really think you can come over here with your crazy food fetishes and yo-yo diets and expect me to take you back?"

I hesitated. Yes, I did think that. "I had to see if this was it, I had to have one last fling to make sure you were my one true love."

"You can't just run off with some guy to see if you want to marry me. What if I did that? What if I started screwing some random woman to see if I love you?"

"Well, you could do that, but only to punish me for hurting you and wouldn't you rather have something to hold over me for the rest of our lives instead? Wouldn't you rather be made up to by me than make out with some girl who couldn't possibly love you like I do?"

He couldn't help but see the logic of this argument, or at least I didn't think he could but he withstood it pretty well. His mouth refused to relax. There was really only one thing left for me to try. I pulled off my shirt. I walked into the kitchen, leaving bra and jeans and underwear along the hall. Naked, I began to bake.

He followed me, of course, and stood watching while I stirred milk and eggs into a mix of lemon poppy seed muffins. I held the bowl against my breasts, moving his long-handled wooden spoon in slow circles. He will never love another woman, I thought, and his gaze upon my face confirmed it.

I woke up the next morning with him curled against my back, our ankles crossed. He was still asleep, breathing into my neck, and I lay there with disturbing thoughts. A path extended before me. He would marry me if I behaved myself. He was looking for peace and stability from a reasonable, intelligent woman. I could be that. We would have children, he wanted two, very soon. Before he turned thirty-five. I saw twenty years extending before me of passive contentment—of course I'd love our children. He'd take care of me. I could go back to school and figure out something to do with my life, something that wouldn't keep me from his laundry but was fulfilling enough to prevent me from going crazy. I could stop sliding from silly job to sillier job, living diet to diet. Boyfriend to lover. I would only have to fit myself into the role of his ideal mate and have it all. He'd pay all the bills, he'd be pleased to maintain me. I'm cheap, I've had to be, floating around. Free.

He shifted and snored a little and gripped me harder around the waist. I slid cautiously out of his arms and off the bed. "Where are you going?" Shit, he was awake. "For donuts," I said. I dressed and kissed him good-bye and barely noticed his mouth against mine because as I said the word, a contentment passed through me, an almost religious conviction. Donuts. I drove past three All Star Donuts, one Rainbo Donut Shoppe and went to the Dunkin' Donuts near my apartment. I'd noticed it the day before. WANTED, the sign in the window said, Responsible, experienced cashier. I went in and smiled warmly at the man behind the counter.

He wasn't bad looking.

Amanda Kenny of Milwaukee, Wisconsin is a graduate student in English Literature and an instructor of Expository Writing for first year college students.

"Yo-yo Girl" was inspired while working as a receptionist for a food service broker. "I wrote the first draft literally between phone calls, shoving my legal pad underneath my blotter whenever anyone walked by my desk." However, while the experience of that job and some of the people she worked with provided the starting point for the story, she would like to emphasize that the rest is fiction.

WAR FARE

In the shadows of the forest, the man felt safe. The soldiers who had been there yesterday would be gone today, for they didn't like the discomfort of a wet forest; not when the neighboring village in the valley below offered women with warm beds. It had been two years since this village had had anything to offer any soldier, and yet the battle still raged, for there was a sense of purpose in gaining territory, even if the land that was won was dead. This land was not dead yet, though; not as long as the man and his family, and his neighbors and their families kept breathing. He stepped more determinedly as he thought of how the land was still his; it had been his family's for five hundred years and did not belong to the soldiers who had been here yesterday. That was why they carried guns.

The trail sloped off, and he moved more quickly now, unwilling to fight the tug of gravity when there were so many other battles still to be fought. He stopped abruptly at the edge of the forest. Autumn light shone in a clearing beyond. He listened, turning at the snapping of a twig only to see that an emaciated dog was watching him from a distance. Another twig snapped, and he looked up. A girl ran down the embankment toward him, barefoot and wrapped in a tattered shawl; a thin girl with a gaunt face and big, dark eyes.

"Papa," she whispered hoarsely. "Will you catch one today?"

The man put a finger to his lips as he peered out into the clearing and to a body of water beyond.

The girl slid up beside her father and took a can of worms from his hand. She tossed her blond hair to one side as she poked among the worms. "You know, the Bilics eat these."

"Bah, the Bilics," Papa replied. "Let them eat worms. We're going to eat fish."

The two slipped out of the forest together into an outcropping of rock, ducking low as they settled upon a wet log.

"But Papa, you never catch anything."

"Today I will, Sejla."

"You can't even reach the water from here," Sejla replied as she looked across the expanse of pebbles to the receded shoreline.

Papa took a rude fishing pole from between two rocks and fitted a tortured worm onto its hook. "You wait and see." He flicked the pole, and the hook and worm set sail toward the water's edge. The hook then stopped, but the worm kept going, landing with a plunk upon the still waters.

"Oh, Papa. You're just feeding the fish for free."

Papa said nothing as he drew the line back in. He fitted another worm to the hook and flicked the pole once more. This time the worm held and landed in the lake with a satisfying splash.

"It's too bad General Milo blew the dam," Sejla mused. "Petar and I would like to swim again someday, before we forget how. But I don't suppose we could get out there now."

Papa's face darkened. "Don't you dare try," he hissed. "The snipers would get you and Petar both."

"But sometimes I wonder if that wouldn't be better." She saw the pained look on her father's face and stood to wrap her arms about his shoulders. "Oh Papa, you know I don't mean that."

A shot rang out. The bullet struck the nearby rock, sending shards of granite whistling past Papa's and Sejla's ears.

"Ow," Sejla cried and dropped quickly to the ground. A trickle of blood formed near her wrist as she held her hand out toward her father.

"Sejla," Papa shouted as he lunged to her side. He grabbed her shoulders and held her up, anxiously scanning her clothes for further signs of blood. "Are you shot?"

"I don't think so, Papa," Sejla replied, frowning at the spot of red as she caressed it with her fingertip. "It was just a sliver of rock."

"We better go, anyway," he whispered, and pushed Sejla's head closer to the ground. "The snipers will give us no peace now that they know we're here."

Sejla crept along beside her father to the forest's edge, then scurried into the underbrush as two more shots rang out. "Do you think they're shooting each other now?"

"We can only hope," Papa replied as he rose to his feet and brushed the dirt from his knees. He helped Sejla to her feet, and the two set off along the path.

"I'm sorry I stood up back there," Sejla remarked as they reached the top of the embankment. "I ruined your fishing."

"We'll still eat," Papa replied. "Mama bought some potatoes from Mrs. Bringa last night."

"Really? Is that why Grandmama's antique clock was missing this morning?"

Winter passed, but its cruelty persisted. A light snow fell upon the small crowd as they stood before an open field, looking anxiously into the sky.

"Do you see it, Petar?" Sejla asked.

A young boy stood nearby, shielding his eyes from the falling flakes. He wore an adult's coat and adult boots that hid the thinness of his body. "Not yet," he replied.

"The radio said noon," Sejla complained.

"Did it say what day, though?" Petar replied distractedly.

"Oh, Petar!" But before Sejla could say more, the drone of a distant engine silenced her.

A woman holding a baby pointed toward the far mountains, but said nothing. It was Mrs. Bringa; and she wished now for the potatoes she had sold last fall. If the plane was real, though, that would no longer matter and there would be food enough for all.

Others pointed too as the drone of the engine grew louder. A woman began to clap. "Oh, I see it," she shouted. A grin spread across her weary face as the dark outline of a cargo plane materialized within the swirling snow. But then, just as quickly, a bright light raced through the sky to greet it, and the woman's smile faded as an erupting ball of orange filled the sky.

"But they said they would let it through," an elderly man shouted, waving a crooked stick at the dying airplane.

"And you trust General Milo?" another man retorted, turning in disgust and trudging through the gathering snow toward the village's last remaining roof.

"Look!" Mrs. Bringa shouted.

The others turned in time to see a half-open parachute separate from the shower of burning wreckage. It spun wildly and landed in the nearby field with a dull thud. The crowd stared unbelieving as the parachute fluttered noisily beside the broken remnants of a wooden crate.

"There's food there," Mrs. Bringa whispered. She stepped forward from between the two buildings that had served to shelter the small crowd.

"Don't," someone shouted. "The truce is off."

"There's food," Mrs. Bringa repeated, walking faster as she pressed her baby against her ribs.

The other's watched. The braver ones took tentative steps forward as Mrs. Bringa approached the broken crate unmolested. They scanned the nearby hills for the glint of a sniper barrel, but saw nothing.

"There's food!" she shouted as she knelt beneath the fluttering parachute, thrusting cans of chocolate syrup up into the swirling snow.

The others began to run out to join her, shouting to one another, "there's food," as they bounded across the gathering snow— but then a sniper shot stopped them in their tracks.

"There's food," Mrs. Bringa whispered once more, then slumped over on her side as her neighbors scurried back to safety between the two buildings.

The villagers looked out across the lonely field, but Mrs. Bringa did not move. Her baby, who had cried steadily for days only to grow silent that morning when it finally accepted that the pain in its stomach was the way life would be; that baby now sat beside its mother, flapping its little arms in quiet protest.

Sejla took a step toward the open field where the baby sat, but her father placed a hand upon her shoulder and stopped her. "Don't," he said. "Snipers."

As the crowd dispersed, returning in twos and threes to their shattered homes, a dog watched the baby hungrily from the forest. That night there was howling in the woods, and in the morning, both Mrs. Bringa and her infant were gone.

"They say the Bilics are eating dead soldiers," Sejla sniffed. She sat beside her father in their dank basement. Artillery shells whistled overhead, and the ground shook while Petar squatted nearby, spooning water onto his mother's white lips.

"Oh, hush," Papa snapped. "No one's eating anybody."

"It's true," Sejla replied. "You can smell the barbecue when the wind's just right."

"That's the soldier's bivouac you smell," Papa suggested.

"It's the Bilics," Sejla argued. "Sometimes I can see the smoke coming from their chimney."

"Last year you said it was worms. This year they're eating people. Don't be grim," Papa sighed.

"Life's grim," Sejla shouted. "Poor Mrs. Bringa laying out there for a whole day, and no one would help her."

"She was dead."

"But what about the baby?"

"The baby would have died, too. There's no milk."

"Well, who started this stupid war, anyway?" Sejla cried.

Papa grew silent as he thought back through the hungry winters. Who had started the war, and why? There must have been a good reason back then to justify such suffering now, but the reason escaped him. There was just war now. He looked sadly at Petar as the boy hummed quietly, running a damp cloth across his mother's forehead. Soon he would be old enough, and General Milo or General Bonac—whichever came first—would add him to their competing army. Perhaps he would be made a sniper and shoot at desperate fishermen as they huddled along the dusty lake bed. There was a time when the boys took sides and knew which army they would join, but news was so rare now, and memories so vague that the boys just waited in fear for someone to grab them off the street and tell them which side was right.

A shell fell on the Dovjak's house across the street. The family had long been dead, and it seemed fitting that the house would finally die, too. Dust poured into the basement among Papa and the others as the Dovjak's great chimney crashed onto the unpaved street.

"Papa? Papa?" Mama called vaguely. "Should Petar be in school?"

"No school today," Papa replied softy. "It's a holiday. Hear the fireworks?"

Mama grew silent as Petar dabbed her cheeks with the damp cloth. A burst of machine-gun fire indicated that the fighting had moved onto the streets.

"The Bilics will have a feast tonight," Sejla remarked.

"Quiet," Papa ordered. "No one in this village is eating humans. It's just not... done."

Petar stood and walked to his father's side. He handed him the damp cloth and sat down heavily in the nearby dirt.

"Your mama's sleeping?" Papa asked.

"She won't be needing me anymore," the boy replied quietly, casting a glance over his shoulder toward his mother's still body.

Papa looked too, and saw his wife's stillness. He wanted to cry, but he felt the hollowness in his belly and sensed that it had invaded his soul, too; that in a final desperate act, his hungry body had devoured all emotion. He patted his son's back and smiled grimly as he felt the sharp bones straining against the boy's skin. The boy had an escape, at least. He could join the army—either army—and be well-fed. And Sejla—well, she could go to the village below and... she'd get fed, at least. It was the older people who had no choices, no escape. Papa looked at his wife and tried to think of a time before the war, when she was so beautiful and the children were so plump, but his memory failed him, and he could only think of the weeks spent huddled in basements, eating rodents and seed pods that were better off planted—if only their hunger weren't so real. He recalled Petar running down the street with two other boys— the day before the two boys disappeared—throwing rocks at an ill-fated crow that had recalled the bountiful gardens that once bloomed in the village and had returned to steal corn, only to become prey himself. He thought of how light his wife had been when he last carried her into the basement. He looked at Sejla and bit his lip when he saw that she was just as thin as her mother.

"Listen," Petar whispered, pointing toward the world above. The artillery lay silent, and after a final burst of gunfire, the streets were quiet, too.

"Stay here," Papa commanded as he rose to his feet. Cautiously, he climbed the fragile ladder to the house above. Their home still stood. Several bricks lay scattered across the living room floor; tossed through the front window by the Dovjak's dying chimney. The front door stood open, and Papa went to close it. A dead soldier lay on their doorstep, well-fed and sporting a crisp, clean uniform. Papa grabbed the dead man's feet and started dragging him toward the backyard where so many others were buried, but then he stopped. The fireplace loomed empty at the back of the kitchen, its dark kettles hanging unused for two long months. His children squatted in the basement below, their youth stolen by hunger, and his wife lay dead beside them. And it was this man who had done it. He had brought the war here. The villagers had not asked them to come. This had always been a peaceful village where men fought only sporadically over goats and other men's wives.

Papa spun the dead man around in the dust. He scanned the street for neighbors, but saw that the others had not yet left their basements. Struggling, he dragged the soldier through the open doorway, trying to ignore how much heavier the man felt now that they were headed toward the kitchen's hollow fireplace and not to the graveyard out back.

David Tillman is the author of several books, including *In the Failing Light,* the memoirs of his wife's seven-year battle with terminal breast cancer, and *Finding Woodstock,* a satire of modern suburban life. His humorous fiction has appeared in naughty men's magazines, such as *Swank* and *Genesis.*

"War Fare" was inspired by news accounts of the many civil wars that continue to plague the planet. Although the setting of the story seems to be the Balkans, Mr. Tillman says he was moved more by tales of the chronic wars of northern Africa when he wrote the story, but put it in a European setting so that it would seem closer to home.

THE BEZALOO

The news of Martín DeSelva's tragedy reached the Miahuatlan Mountains in January. His friends and campesinos were mortified. DeSelva was the most honorable of men, and for a man of honor to be thrown onto the Periferico Highway with two hundred chickens shitting in his face was an insult impossible to bear.

Furthermore, his beautiful wife, Rosa Salanueva, was taken from him, as well as two fine boys, Erriberto and Eduardo, maimed and crushed with deliberate wantonness.

The oldest man in all the Miahuatlan villages, Adelaido Golpe, claimed that on the night of the accident, a pillar of black clouds rose in the sky to choke the moon. Shepherd boys, rounding up goats on the curve of the mountain face, sickened when they smelled green gas fouling the air.

Miahuatlanos are keen trackers, with uncanny abilities to hunt by smell. They can sniff the spoors of a puma long after the puma's climbed into the rocks and disappeared. They can tell you where the puma's heading, when it will get there, if it wants be alone and sulk, or circle back and kill for the sport of killing. In the cities below, white skinned *Gachupino* Catholics consider this a magic, a witchcraft, but in the mountains it is merely a skill, a practicality. Zapotecan peoples cock their fingers in the form of a jest, and claim they can smell a *bezaloo* lurking in the shadows.

"Don Martín DeSelva," Miahuatlanos would say to him when he

180

was growing up to be the leader they wanted him to be, "the bezaloo belongs to all of us."

Admired from one end of the Sierras to the Istmo of Tehuantepac, far away Tehuanos sold him oil and machines, and in return, bought his grain, goats, and fruits, on a handshake alone. If Martín DeSelva gave you his word, it was as good as money in the bank and gold in the ground. In a land where most rich folk were hard as flint, with hearts inured to poor people's sufferings, here was a *hacendado* who loaned you money when you could not pay your bills, sent your children to fancy schools, and paid their upkeep. Don Martín DeSelva treated you like an equal. Many said it was more like a brother. On his hacienda it was known that the poorest, blackest Indio swallowed the wafer side by side the richest, whitest Gachupino Catholic. This was a rarity in Mexico. But then he was a rare man. When the news of the tragedy reached the people of the Miahuatlan, they fell to their knees in consternation and prayed. "What crimes have we committed? What sin must we repent?"

They pried into their hearts, but all they could dredge up from the past were the sweetest images of an honorable life. Martín DeSelva and Rosa Salanueva were married in the Dominican chapel in central Oaxaco. It is true they could have chosen the great cathedral there, with spiraling vaults and massive ceilings, but they picked the adobe chapel for its simplicity. It was a simple time then, a much more simple time, when people were content with their lives. It was remembered that God's light streamed across the adobe walls, showering people with a gentle radiance.

All the villagers were invited to the wedding feast. In the traditional way of the Zapotecas, the wedding party began as the sun was descending, and stars were rising in the sky. The bride and the groom were seated on palm mats, and Daria Obregon, the *great curandera* of the mountains, tied their shirts together. It was she who raised DeSelva when he was orphaned as a boy, and now this old, old lady brought them *copas of tepache* and bade them drink.

She prayed, loudly, and proudly, and "Bless all here," and then she kissed Martín's hands and wept tears of happiness. She kissed Rosa's hands, and without embarrassment, embraced her as a daughter. Church bells rang in celebration. Friends and campesinos remembered how the night was clear, and that a breeze swept the mountains clean.

Miahuatlanos are cynical people. They rarely sing of happiness, or concern themselves with lasting enjoyment; their vision of the world plays out within a series of miseries, replete with betrayal. They expect bad things to happen, and that is ordinary fate; but they will not abide insulting kinds of death, for the difference between ordinary good and ordinary evil is the insult.

The accident occurred December 23rd, 1949, just as the century was reaching the middle of its life, the moment when Zapotecan prophecies predicted explosive evil. Of course, prophecies are used and abused, and mocked at, throughout the Miahuatlan.

The Salanueva DeSelvas were on a holiday in the market town of Cholula, celebrating the *Noche de Rabanes,* the Night of the Radishes, a time for Mardi Gras, for gallows humor mocking customs and Mother Church. Evil and Death were costumed as silly puppets, puffed up with pride, dancing on a string, to be kicked at and punched by giggling children.

Cholula was crowded and alive with thrumming music. People danced in the streets. A host of mariachi bands trumpeted *corridas* and love songs. The *zocalo* was decorated with skulls and bones made from papier maché and cotton candy. The streets were illuminated with candles and flaming torches.

In preparation for the main event, Cholula farmers 'played' with their radishes for a full year, stretching them and pulling at their fibers until the radishes reached gigantic shapes and sizes. At a prearranged signal, mariachi bands blew their trumpets and beat their drums. 'Stunted children,' as farmers called the freak radishes, marched through the center of town as if they were warriors. Firecrackers exploded, and black powder bombs fizzled in the night with a wheezing and a sobbing until great pillars of smoke billowed through the air and the zocalo looked like a war zone.

"Poppa," Erriberto whispered, "look! They're crying out. They're moving."

Martín had to hold the boy in his arms and reassure him. The radishes were as twisted and bizarre as any demon, with roots and veins bursting with blood.

"Unnatural," Eduardo whispered. "This is sacrilege."

"No, no," Rosa said, calming her children, "merely fun and games. It happens once a year, like a puff of smoke, and goes away. So learn to live with it. Forgive it."

"I can't, momma... this is... *an infamia...*"

"An infamia?... as much as that?"

"It's unnatural, momma... and seriously wrong."

"I'd like you to listen to me," Rosa said to her children. "Does it grow in the ground?" she argued politely.

"Yes, it grows in the ground?"

"Does God make the ground?"

"Yes, God makes the ground."

"Is God all around us?"

"God is everywhere."

"Then wouldn't you say that what comes from the ground is God's order?"

"But this is evil."

"'Why is it evil?"

"Because it doesn't look right."

"Sometimes you don't look right. Are you evil?"

"Momma," Eduardo smiled at his mother, "evil is evil."

"Does God create vile people?"

"Ah ha, he has you there," Martín crowed, enjoying his son's acuity.

"Are you saying God creates bad things?" Rosa replied, proud of

Eduardo's jousting.

"I know these radishes are vile... and they sicken me."

"Behave yourself," Rosa admonished. "God will hear you."

"Gentlemen," Martín addressed his two sons, "your mother is a Jesuit."

"Oh no, momma is not a Jesuit. She is a *Tejacoqui!* "Erriberto said, proclaiming for all the world to hear that Rosa Salanueva was a Zapotecan princess, and that when you come from the Tejacoqui, claro, you are sharp, and clever. You ask the kind of questions and you deal with the kind of answers that Gachupino Catholics are afraid to uncover.

"Truly, momma," Eduardo continued, "I think it's most disturbing."

"Most disturbing," DeSelva said, gently mocking his oldest son. "Eduardo, you sound like an Englishman."

"These radishes... smell of death... I don't understand the fun of it... or why people do it..."

"It is an unfortunate truth, my son, that dying takes the fun out of life. Truly!"

Eduardo stared at his father, and then he laughed, as he had been taught to laugh, at the madness, himself, the hysterical music exploding in his ears. As the parade of stunted children swirled by his side, pummeling him with blows to the head, and as the music thrummed and bombs went off in the air, Erriberto embraced his father.

"Am I an old maid, then," Rosa said, "to be left in the cold?"

"Erriberto is right," Eduardo said, holding his mother up to the light, as if he were a grown man. "You *are* a princess!"

Jaws broken, body mummified in plaster, Martín DeSelva murmured these snatches of dialogue—far away memories—to his brother-in-law, Antonio Salanueva, sitting by his side. So many deaths? So many horrors? All those fucking chickens on the highway, squawking in blood? Madre de Deus, God in heaven, for the life of him, Antonio Salanueva could not understand what he was hearing, where was he, for God's sake? He lifted his head, trying to suck in a breath of fresh air, as if he, too, were being crushed by a drunken chicken farmer from Cholula.

For the longest time, Antonio crouched by Martín's side, sick to his stomach, rocking backwards and forwards, unable to swallow. He dripped spittle onto the hospital floor and continued to spit, hour after hour, until a rivulet circled his feet.

Antonio was Rosa's brother and protector. A humorless man, Rosa's smile made him feel life was viable. She would never smile again. And poor Erriberto, Eduardo. He was their *compadre,* a true compadre in the old mountain way; he loved them more than he did his own children, for they were something special, like their father.

Antonio and Martín were lifelong friends and business partners. They trusted each other, implicitly. In a world that expected betrayal and broken trust, theirs was a friendship that was sung about in the ballad songs of the Miahuatlan. Although physically and spiritually dissimilar, they had learned to fit into each other's skin and work within each other's boundaries.

Salanueva was a massive man, with a thick head mounted on a muscular body. His hands were shaped like hammers, and behind his back, the smaller Miahuatlanos called him "Ox." He paid his campesinos good wages, excellent wages, but when they got drunk, or they wasted their time on the 'lying dice,' (for Miahuatlanos practice lying and cheating even in their games of chance) Antonio offered them little patience. He showed them his horns. There was nothing subtle about his personality. He was as direct as a blow to the head. Ox suited him, for in the Miahuatlan, the ox is a most admired animal.

Salanueva sat, stood up again, paced the room, spitting and shaking, overwhelmed by the news, and now he looked down at his brother-in-law and friend, this frail, courtly man, wrapped in a body cast, mouth wired, barely able to speak, plumes of blood and saliva seeping between his lips, lying in this hell of pain and death, murmuring about radishes and evil and what is natural and what is not unnatural until Antonio Salanueva actually smelled stench in the room, as if he himself understood the meaning of this rot. "My poor friend," he said, smelling the bezaloo. "Oh, my poor friend... we have killing to do."

DeSelva's right hip bone was shattered. His right thigh, knee cap, and tibia suffered deep lacerations. There was massive internal hemorrhaging. The midshaft of the ulna and radius was fractured. When that chicken farmer from Cholula hurtled through space and time like an exploding bomb, smashing into the DeSelva family, Martín had thrown his arms up in front of his face to save himself— and so he deserved the pain. He deserved it. And as a curse for his cowardice, forevermore, he would see the mouth of that farmer screaming insanities, and that would be his future, year after year of insult.

When he was young, DeSelva studied with anthropologists from the Oaxacan Valley. Skeletons of human beings were uncovered near the hills of his hacienda. Some were old, some not so old. Experts agreed the earth where all the bones lay hidden was not a burial ground in the normal sense of the meaning, but a dumping place for executed hostages. There were so many fractures of the right ulna and radius, anthropologists called them "parry fractures," as if the hostages were vying to ward off blows of a machete, or the strikes of a bezaloo.

Not for one instant did his friends and campesinos believe the accident an ordinary blow of fate. Claro, these deaths were malevolent. Some vile thing had 'calculated' them. If the good Martín DeSelva could no longer raise his arm and fight back in noble revenge, his people would do it for him, in the method and style of the Miahuatlan Mountains; they would wait until the time was right, be it a moment, a year, or a decade, but Madre de Deus, they would execute that bezaloo, and the insult would be repaid a thousand times over.

All life, Miahuatlanos reasoned, is fraught with treachery. Alliances molder. Morals corrupt. Even one's great love diminishes. This is commonplace, work of the laughing gods. This is to be expected, routinely expected, but when the mocking spirits expand and grow into something vile, when the insults metastasize into something monstrous, claro, one cannot fight this evil alone. It is folly to fight evil alone. Collectively, then, with the will of the people, you must spit into the bezaloo's face and show it you are worthy. That is the way it's always been done, and so it was that the people of the Miahuatlan came down from the mountains to visit Don Martín as he lay dying in the hospital.

For many days and nights they journeyed to Mexico City to hold his hand and bring him presents. They brought him what they could, for they were plain people, who held their hats in their hands and lowered their eyes when they spoke to you. Unsophisticated and alarmed by the noises of Mexico City, they were bedeviled by engines belching smoke into the air. Everywhere they turned, there were stinks and vile smells.

Their journey was an arduous probe into unfamiliar ground, and expensive. Antonio Salanueva could have paid for their fare, he was rich enough, but this would have been insulting to the campesinos, who believed that everyone had to pay whatever they could, and in this way, their united passion would save a good man.

On the first day of the week, Monday, usually reserved for market, Miahuatlano visitors brought Don Martín packages of acorns and almonds. On Tuesdays, there were *tejocate* apples, the kind he loved to eat when he was a boy. He'd slice them into little pieces, fill his cheeks as if he were a squirrel, then suck out the juices. On Wednesday, his visitors brought him fruits from his own *zapote* trees, as if the trees and the man who had planted them thirty years ago would go on living forever. Even then, in the Miahuatlan, the zapote tree was a dying breed, but incredibly, as a source of wonder and a sign to his campesinos, his zapote trees were flowering. Especially now were they flowering. Thursdays, his friends brought good things to eat, tamales wrapped in banana leaves, sweet breads made with cornmeal and a dozen eggs; also there were rejuvenative soups, filled with meat and chicken. The smells were from his faraway childhood, when he played in the kitchen of his cook, Daria Obregon, learning the culinary arts of Oaxaca, for not only was she the overseer of all his campesinos, she was the most noted chef in the Miahuatlan.

On Fridays, Daria Obregon sent the patient mountain gourds stuffed with marigolds and dried crocuses. On Saturdays, there were wattled baskets filled with orange blossoms, spikenard, and quince. On Sundays, his hospital room blazed with the flowery reds, whites, and greens of the Miahuatlan Mountains. This was the day, too, when visitors brought Daria's famous tangerine drinks, the ones she mixed with secret spices. The visitors would not leave his bedside until they had seen him swallow these sacred elixirs. Then they would return to the mountains and tell Daria Obregon, in the minutest of details, how the patient had been a good boy and drunk everything to the last drop. And as they spoke, described what they had observed, the old woman wept and scratched her skin.

Daria Obregon raised Martín DeSelva when most of his relatives perished in the Revolution; it was she who held his cheeks between her hands and called him "Mijo," my son. In most parts of Mexico, when a servant called her master 'my son,' she would've been beaten on the spot, kicked like a common cur. The shock! Perhaps it was due to the fact Zapotecas ate wheat breads more often than corn, and lived in the high places, or that Daria Obregon, herself, was descended from the *Tijacoqui*. In the Miahuatlan, a great curandera succeeds on merit alone, on the number of animals cured and patients healed, not on some fancy reputation, or Gachupino shingle. Almost seventy years of healing had given her a formidable will and the eye of a prophet. Not many people would stand in her way. It's true she was shriveled and bent over, and only one eye worked, but that eye, Madre de Deus, flashed with lightening. When she opened her toothless jaw to speak, out snaked the tongue of a lizard, ready to strike your face if you showed her disrespect.

Martín DeSelva lingered between life and death for three months. In his ever-present morphia dreams, he whispered nightly to his wife, "Rosa... I want to die... I'm ready... come for me." His campesinos would not listen to these prayers or let him slide away so easily.

Miahuatlanos slash at death; they swing their machetes; they jab and hook their knives until death grows weary and tries to flee; or once and for all, reaches out and grips you by the throat and drags you off to his cave. In the mountains, claro, one does not give up. It is not proper to give up. Life is taken from you.

The great Gringo War was over, and news of its bestialities were reaching the Miahuatlan Mountains. It was as if the Zapotecan prophesies were coming to fruition. It was clear to the people of the mountains an uncommon evil was sweeping the faraway world, yes, there, taking over the outside world, but here in the Miahuatlan? Never! Never here! For when people are clever, and considerate, and apologize for mistakes, evil journeys elsewhere.

Towards the beginning of April, when nights and days were un-usually hot, the old curandera awoke with a start and discovered she had fallen out of bed. A layer of sweat drenched her body. Blood pounded through her head. A stink was in the room, the incredible stench of a bezaloo, trapped by four walls closing in on it, and now it was squealing, crazed by its impotence to flee, to escape through the windows, to slip under the cracks of the door and escape into the night. Daria Obregon could feel her heart jabbing her chest. She sat on the edge of her bed and called on all the forces of her life to help her battle the stench. Placing a pinch of tobacco between her lips and gums, she waited for the mixture to salivate so she could spit. Sometimes, answers to problems are right in front of your own nose. Sometimes these answers are so simple to achieve, it's hard to believe they come without a struggle. And because the vision of it came to her quickly, it took her breath away, and she did not trust it. But the more she deliberated, and the more she spat at the bezaloo, crawling and groveling in the corner, the more she grew accustomed to its evil. Daria Obregon would create a giant feast, a *grand guzon*. She dreamed it, and at the same time, she created it, and made it live. She would overwhelm the bezaloo with human kindness and largess; she would stuff its hunger and its madness with as much food as it could eat, until the beast was so swollen with the fruits of nature it would barely be able to move, or belch. So disgraced, it would try to escape, with its tail tucked between its legs. Then, at the height of its fear and self contempt, DeSelva's friends and campesinos would piss on it, condemn it, and drive it away with the combined strength of human righteousness.

So it was that with the help of Antonio the Ox, horse and rider were dispatched to the highest places of the Miahuatlan, announcing the news of a great guzon. Broadsheets were printed, and all were invited to attend. Father Tommasso would sing midnight mass; old folks would chant the hymns of *Teonactle*. Younger choristers would praise the Blessed Virgin.

Miahuatlanos would then form a candle-lit procession, and starting from the base of DeSelva's hacienda, move into the mountains, climbing higher and higher until the people could go no further, then turning around, descend into the towns below, through all the secret passageways known to the Zapotecan tribes, illuminating darkness, the night, for a friend who needed prayers.

Daria Obregon had never married. She was childless. She did, however, have three fine nieces, who were fond of her and she of them, and the curandera made sure the secrets of the old Zapotecan ways would not perish when she was carried away by death. It was part of her life's work to teach her nieces everything she knew, and they obeyed her, and listened, for it was an honor to be instructed by one so wise. It was announced, as a symbolic gesture, that she and the three fine nieces would pay for this guzon with their own funds. Furthermore, they would only make the foods DeSelva himself loved to eat. However, if people felt the urge to help in the undertaking, naturally they could 'give to the kettle.'

In the beginning of their days together, it was her duty to introduce DeSelva to the intricacies of her kitchen. She taught him how to pluck feathers and scramble eggs. She taught him the power of a sharp knife, and how to quiet squealing pigs. Her job was to teach him the ways of the world, and O Teonactle, there is much to learn, and most men are stupid. In time, this four-year-old boy, scampering through her kitchen and banging her pots and pans, would be a wise person, a leader.

The first course she dreamed, then served at the great guzon, was a mighty beef *quizado,* and the very first dish DeSelva had learned to master. He was taught how to pound the meat, grill it swiftly with a little oil, place it into the stew pot, add tomatoes, chilies, sugar and salt, then throw in the fiery peppers and spices of the mountains. The stew was simmered until it was shiny as the sea, and redolent with the great smells and memories of fresh earth.

Next came two kinds of *pozoles,* one shredded with pork and marinated in hominy and spices, and the other, a cubed pork, made drunken with herbs and glistening corn. *Pozoles* were the specialties of the Miahuatlan; Daria made hers with wild mountain pig. A domestic pig was not good enough. Adelaido Golpe led young Martín up into the secret places so he could learn about the wily animal, what it ate, what it drank, where and when it disappeared into the ground. It was hard to hunt and harder to kill, but once it was dressed and popped into the pot, Madre de Deus, O Teonactle, the taste was sublime.

Next on her dream list came another Oaxacan specialty, *guzanos de maguey,* white maggots that wriggled on the cactus plants. In the beginning of his lessons, Martín ran around the cookhouse floor swearing he would never eat those stinking things of merda, they were disgusting, completely unnatural. They were slimy, and vile, but when Daria fried them up a golden brown, they tasted just like bacon. And when the guzanos were served on tortillas made of wheat, with an interior bed of crisp lettuce, God in heaven, what a treat!

In the mountains of Oaxaca, it is a well known fact that wheat eaters are a different breed of people altogether, claro. Wheat eaters, unlike corn eaters, do not bow, or scrape, nor do they ever forget an insult. That is why their dreams are always stimulating, and why they are not allowed to die whimpering in bed, accepting *infamies.*

"Skin the *nopal,*" Daria commanded, teaching Martín the intricacies of the cactus dish. "Pay attention! Do not look away. Chop its heart into little pieces. Do not make fun of it. Sing songs of admiration so the heart smiles at you and gives you its love, its respect. Now mix it with diced potatoes. Add these flecks of rosemary, these strings of garlic. Throw in the dried shrimps from the Gulf Coast. Cover this beautiful, sleeping princess with a blanket of beaten eggs. Bake her! Believe in her! Thus, we will create when the dish is done, the finest marriage in our kitchen."

One more cactus dish was dreamed and served by Daria and her three nieces, *nopales navigantes,* an ancient food of the gods considered *muy antigas,* and ceremonially important to the Zapotecas. "If I were to die," Daria Obregon told her nieces, "you will live on after me to cook the old ways. If you die, then Martín DeSelva will make these *navigantes,* but if I die, and you die, and he passes, then it will be over for the mountain peoples and all our secrets will disappear."

It was hard work skinning the cactus, scraping the insides, chopping the nopales into small pieces, placing the meat into large ceramic bowls to ferment in the sun; then the mixture was dropped ever so carefully into boiling vats of tomato broth, along with chopped chilies, followed by cilantro, lemon juice, salt, and secret spices. The dried chilies burned Martín's skin when he crushed them between his palms. He had to use all of his strength to make them yield their mysteries. The odor and the mist of the chilies made his eyes weep, until the three nieces laughed at him with a sweet delight, and consoled his crying in the kitchen by saying, "Learning is never important unless it burns!"

There came a time when Adelaido Golpe dispatched the young hunter into the hills all by himself to hide, watch, and spring into action, returning with the rarest piece of meat in all the world, the *cachicamo*. The mountain armadillo spends most of its life hidden under ground. Its taste is so prized, it's been hunted to the point of extinction. Tonight, the night of the great guzon, in memory of old times and old friends, cachicamo was served side by side the fillets of the broiled caguamo turtle from the southern Istmo. Gray flesh and green meat symbolized unity.

Surrounding the cachicamo were pieces of toasted *pinoles,* kernels of corn that were popped into the fire and dipped in salt. Many a night the orphaned Martín slept with a hoard of pinoles wrapped tightly in his fist, trying to remember what his mother looked like, for she, too, loved pinoles. She'd chew them slowly and politely, and with a loving smile, offer him a taste.

When the body bloats from rich food, Miahuatlanos revive themselves with drinks famous to the mountains. So it was that Daria Obregon served her fine *tejate,* a mixture of cacao, flowers, and water, marinated for three days and nights. Once, Martín ran circles around the tejate, stomping his feet and crying out, "Is it done? It must be done. This is done!" On the second day of the marinating, he ran into the kitchen howling, "Why isn't it done? It must be done! I want to taste it." But on the third day, chastened, and wary, he sat by the tejate mixture and eyed it ever so carefully, determined to master his impatience. When Daria said at last, "Drink. Now it's done!" he said, "Oh, no. It needs more time!" How the nieces loved that story. They repeated it many times during the great guzon.

Chilacayota is made from pumpkins, and it is a drink that spreads through the body with narcotic sweetness. It is not wise to gorge on Chilacayota, for it makes you defenseless in the presence of evil. To revive the senses, you taste from the simplest of all foods in the Miahuatlan, a pot of black beans, simmered with *ipazote* herbs. It is so wonderful a dish, it is said that even the gods prefer these beans to blood.

There came a time at the end of the great guzon when man, woman, child, beast, could no longer eat another mouthful. *Tequila anejo* and fine *mescal* were poured into clay cups, and the cups were raised in the air. Antonio Salanueva and Daria Obregon stepped forward, orchestrating a mass salute to the guest of honor, lying far away in his hospital bed. People toasted and drank, then hurled their cups against the ground until the cups shattered. The shards were driven into the earth and buried under foot. "This... is in your honor... my Beppie...," the old woman whispered to the skies, calling him by a name she used for a four-year-old scoundrel running around the tejate. It was a name he loved to hear. No one else ever called him by this name, save this withered old crone with one good eye. How magical a name can be... O Teonactle... God in heaven... how magical is the eye that looked after me. Madre de Deus, bless her.

He was in morphia, and he could not move. Of course, the pain was excruciating, and of course, he had cried out, shamefully. Exhausted now, he lay in his dream state, visualizing disintegration. Surely no one could blame him for giving up the ghost. It was time. The sap was oozing from the tree. He was slipping into the stillness of pure, white light, letting go of breath, floating away on a journey of death when he smelled the beans, with ipazote herbs.

A lamb was bleating, tied to a short rope. Then he saw the puma, circling his bed, 'captured' by the gurgling of the lamb's sacrifice, enraged with hunger. O Teonactle, Martín cried out in his dream, my lamb is ready to die. So be it. It is time!

Never! Never!

The craggy face of the curandera pushed on through the caul of the hospital light. Her trembling hands, covered with liver spots, tore a hole in his burial shroud. He could hear the pawing and the scratching coming closer; he felt hot breath against his skin, and he knew she was as real as life, her paws rough as a cachicamo's hide.

"Mijo," she hissed. "Your soul is wandering." The right side of the curandero's mouth dripped with spittle, as if she were taken, and abused, with stroke. It was she who whispered magic words into his ear: "Revenge yourself!"

When he was home from his hospital bed, healing, among his old friends, he was sitting with them around a camp fire, drinking aged tequila and fine mescal when he spoke to them, haltingly, about his dreams, dreams brighter than any reality he had ever experienced. He described to them how an ordinary pot of beans, a common pot of beans with ipazote herbs smelled and tasted richer than any food he had ever eaten. He even described to his friends how an old crone came flying through the air to hold him in her cachicamo paws.

Dreams are ever mysterious things in the Miahuatlan, at once guardedly personal, yet connected to all in the community. There are many people who say that dreams are silly things, and nothing but the detritus of the brain. Others say there is wisdom and merit to be found in them. His old friends respected dreams, feared them, but now they showed not the slightest bit of discomfort. They spat into the fire, and crossed themselves, humorously, as if they were conspirators in a comedic plot. They slapped themselves on the back, cocked their fingers at DeSelva, and for Miahuatlanos, their behavior was positively boisterous. "Old friend," Antonio Salanueva said, rising to his feet, a sly grin on his face, "we have stories of our own to tell thee."

It seems that all the people who had ever been cured, nursed, or fed, by the curandera Daria Obregon, were assembled in the court-yard of the hacienda. They brought her many pesos and garlands of peonies. They brought her ribbons, and pieces of embroidery, which they sewed to her dress. A band played all the old songs, with xylophones and trumpets, and twelve-stringed guitars.

The old lady was then escorted to a *caleche* taxi cab parked in front of the hacienda. The taxi was newly painted, festooned with orange blossoms and spikenard, plaited with leaves of the wild mountain laurel.

Antonio the Ox was there; he lifted the curandera into his arms as if she were a handful of feathers. Then he placed her, ever so gingerly, inside the caleche. He did the same for the three plump nieces, with their pots and pans and bulging baskets of marvelous food. The crowd applauded. This caleche was a magic coach, and it would take the old lady and her three nieces hurtling through space, and time, across the vast colonias of Mexico City to visit her son, and to bring him home.

Daria Obregon had never been to Mexico City. In fact, she had never been anywhere outside of these mountains, so when the caleche taxi cab pitched forward with a squealing burst of speed, the curandera gripped her pot of beans with dear life. Friends cheered. The band played. Children danced alongside the caleche and showered the old lady with garlands of flowers. Touched to the quick, she closed her eyes, and in the old way, and in the new way, she prayed for a journey of life. That was a great day for all of us, when we killed the bezaloo.

––––––––––

Ben Wilensky, Rockaway, NY
Merchant seaman, soldier, news reporter, and art teacher.

"Bezaloo" was inspired by the years his family lived in Mexico.

Fiction From Essex Press

Finding Woodstock
by David Tillman

From *Boulder Weekly* - Built on a foundation of black humor a la Kurt Vonnegut and generously underpinned with jabs at the slow strangulation of life in the suburbs, Tillman's book amuses without giving up any of its pointed barbs. This is an excellent read for those who wonder how anyone living in a lily-white, economically gated community can justify calling themselves a liberal. And it's a call to action—or a requiem—for any aging boomers out there who might have a nagging ghost of a recollection of all they gave up when they started moving up.

From *Publishers Weekly* - Harry Lascome, his wife, Beth, and their two children are just settling into their new home in an unnamed community at the outset of Tillman's breezy send-up of the charms of suburbia.... Harry loses his job and Beth leaves the family to embark on a lesbian affair and road trip with new girlfriend, Eve. Shaken and confused, Harry finds himself named in the will of his lone client, who has left him $8 million provided that he move to her farm and care for her cat. Once at the farm Harry hooks up with some throwbacks to the '60s and, before long, he begins to realize that there's more to life than cold hard cash.... This is sweet, light fare with a refreshingly buoyant attitude toward the unusual life changes of an ordinary American family.

Poetry From Essex Press

Unexpected Light
by Marylin Lytle Barr

Praise For Other Books By Marylin Lytle Barr

Drawn From The Shadows

"It is a rare person who will not respond with pleasure to these visions of far-away hills as well as to the homely realities."
– Robert C. Dentan

"The poet conjures up the sheer sensuality of a moment. She draws on her considerable ability to create a sense of atmosphere that is nearly cinematic in its vividness."
– Gail Bradney

Concrete Considerations

"Marylin Barr is a mature and finished poet.... Her poems are replete with detail that gives the reader a solid sense of reality."
– Yamile Craven

"As an artist as well as poet, Barr is very observant and attuned to her cityscape and time. She uses words to paint the city and its people with a critical and compassionate eye."
– Mary Durham

"Ms. Barr can be common and she can be rare. She can be profound and she can be comfortably superficial. She cannot be insensitive."
– Dusty Dog Review

Fiction From Essex Press

Kahoolies!
by David McKecknie

*D*octor Stricken pointed the ray gun at the professor's bobbing head. "Someone dim the lights, please."

The room darkened. A strange light erupted from the barrel of the doctor's invention, followed by the smell of ozone drifting across the dinner table. The guests sat in silence as in the half-light a glowing green object appeared, shaped more like an orangutan than a man, hanging precariously to the professor's hunched shoulder as he spun slowly upon the table top. The professor himself sat stoically, looking more like a plaster casting than a living, breathing man.

"His soul is rather large," Mitzy remarked. "From the stories I've heard, I would have guessed he had no soul at all."

"I believe the soul is neutral," Doctor Stricken replied, not taking his eyes from the object of his strange experiment. "My guess would be it indicates breadth of experience, and not the moral content of the body."

The door to the kitchen swung open, and Mary entered the dining room carrying a tray of dinner plates. "Lamb's getting cold, Mum, and I did work hard indeed preparing it."

"Yes, yes. We have had enough for now, I suppose." Doctor Stricken flicked off his ray gun and set it on the table, but the professor's soul still hovered on the lazy Susan. The loss of the ray gun's influence only seemed to agitate the poor creature, and he began hopping about as if his green toes were set upon a hot griddle.

"Oh, look! He's doing a little jig." Lena clapped her hands enthusiastically. "Mitzy, you have finally outdone the Rhinebacks for entertainment."

"What the hell?" Doctor Stricken jumped to his feet and thrust a hand out, stopping the lazy Susan in its tracks. It was too late, though. The professor's soul curtsied twice before the delighted Lena, then scooted to the end of the table where it startled George by leaping straight through him. Margaret, finding herself mildly infected by Lena's enthusiasm, clapped cautiously as the little creature continue on toward the kitchen in a series of somersaults, but she gasped when she saw it quickly dissolve into thin air as it reached the swinging door.

AND SO IT BEGAN

ESSEX PRESS
P. O. BOX 914
NORTH ANDOVER, MA 01845

TITLE	PRICE	QUANTITY	TOTAL PRICE
Finding Woodstock	$9.95	_____	_____
Food and Other Enemies	$14.00	_____	_____
Kahoolies!	$12.00	_____	_____
Unexpected Light	$15.00	_____	_____
	MERCHANDIZE TOTAL		_____
	POSTAGE & HANDLING		__FREE__
	SUBTOTAL		_____
	SALES TAX (FOR DELIVERY IN MA ADD 5%)		_____
	TOTAL ORDER		_____

PAYMENT METHOD:
Personal check or money order
payable to D & M Services

MAILING ADDRESS:

NAME_____

STREET ADDRESS_____

CITY_____ **STATE**_____ **ZIP**_____